DOWN IN THE PINEY WOODS

Down in the Piney Woods

>>>>>>>>>>>>>>>>>>>>>>>>>>>>>>>>>>>

Ethel Footman Smothers

 Alfred A. Knopf *New York*

to my father, IRA FOOTMAN,
whom I love very much,
and with special thanks to
my editors,
Frances Foster and
Jonathan Schmidt

This is a Borzoi Book published by Alfred A. Knopf, Inc.

Text copyright © 1992 by Ethel Footman Smothers
Jacket art copyright © 1992 by James Ransome
All rights reserved under International and Pan-American Copyright Conventions. Published in the United States by Alfred A. Knopf, Inc., New York, and simultaneously in Canada by Random House of Canada Limited, Toronto. Distributed by Random House, Inc., New York.

Book design by Mina Greenstein
Manufactured in the United States of America
10 9 8 7 6 5 4 3 2 1

Library of Congress Cataloging-in-Publication Data
Smothers, Ethel Footman. Down in the piney woods /
by Ethel Footman Smothers. p. cm.
Summary: The joys and frustrations of family life are portrayed through the eyes of Annie Rye, the ten-year-old daughter of a black sharecropper.
ISBN 0-679-80360-2 (trade)
ISBN 0-679-90360-7 (lib. bdg.)
[1. Family life—Fiction. 2. Brothers and sisters—Fiction. 3. Afro-Americans—Fiction.] I. Title.
PZ7.S66475Do 1991 [Fic]—dc20 91-328

Author's Note

>>>>>>>>>>>>>>>>>>>>>>>>>>>>>>>>>>>

THE EARLY PART of my childhood was spent in a backwoods section of Georgia known as the Piney Woods. Teacakes, grass dolls, and the rolling store are all special memories from that long-ago time when I was nicknamed Annie Rye, a time when we made up games and were amused by homemade playthings.

Down in the Piney Woods is based on incidents from that unforgettable past and is due in large part to my sister Doris Dudley. She has kept these memories fresh in my mind and continues to keep the family history alive.

Contents

>>>>>>>>>>>>>>>>>>>>>>>>>>>>>>>>>>

DOWN IN THE PINEY WOODS

chapter 1

Rolling Store

≫≫≫≫≫≫≫≫≫≫≫≫≫≫≫≫≫≫≫≫≫≫≫≫≫

"BROTHER . . . BROTHER, wake up." I shakes him some. But he keeps right on sleeping. Mama calls him the knee baby, 'cause he was born before Elouise, who's the baby now. But sometime he act more like a baby than Elouise do. And he going on eight years old.

"Brother, git yourself up." This time I shakes him a lot. "Wake up."

"I don't wanna," he mumbles, with his eyes still shut.

> *"Okay, sleepy head,*
> *Stay in bed.*
> *Wash yo' face wit shortening bread.*

"I'm gon' git ready to meet the rolling store."

"Rolling store!" Brother set straight up, his eyes shining just like marbles. "I gotta find my pennies." And before I know it, he underneath the bed. "Here they is."

Brother empty a paper sack out on the covers. "Lookit all them pennies. I sho got me a heap, don't I, Annie Rye?" he says to me. Nobody calls me by my real name. Annie Moriah. Annie from my grandma on my daddy's side and Moriah from my great-grandma on my mama's side. They just say Annie Rye for short. Just like Brother doing now.

"I'm gonna buy me some jawbone breakers. Annie Rye, what you gon' buy?"

"I might buy me some soda water—Pepsi-Cola or else I might have me one of them RCs."

I got my pennies in a King Edward cigar box. So I take some out and tie them up in one of Mama's head rags. Brother still got his scattered over the covers. "Make haste pick your pennies up, so's I can straighten up your bed."

"Not yet. I gotta count 'em some more."

"Brother, you done counted them pennies more times than a turkey got feathers. If you don't quit, they gonna disappear. And you won't have nary one left when the rolling store comes."

Brother scoop up a handful of pennies and dump them back in the paper sack. "Annie Rye, you just making up a story."

"Naw I'm not neither. One time I heard about a man who kept gazing at something he had till he couldn't see it no more."

"I ain't stud'ing 'bout what you say. I know where my pennies gonna be. Right here in my hand."

I see there is no use trying to talk no sense into Brother's head. So I change my sleeping clothes to my everyday ones, 'cause Mama don't allow nobody to come to her table in what they done slept in all night. And if you aiming to make Mama real mad, you come before you been to the washpan with matter sticking out the corner of your eyes. She'd be all over you like white on rice. She says it don't make no difference about us living here in Climax, Georgia, back in these woods. We still going to act like we civilized.

"You up mighty early this morning. The chickens barely up yet," Mama says to me when I come to the table. "Where's Brother? He up too?"

"Here I is." Brother comes in, holding his paper sack.

"So I see. And what y'all up to, so early in the morning? Annie Rye, I don't want y'all gitting into no kinda devilment. You ten years old, and I spect for you to act like it." Mama got that "I mean what I say" sound in her voice, so I don't waste no time telling her what I meant.

"We won't, Mama. I just wanna have all my work did."

"You know what day this is, Mama? Did you know the rolling store s'pose to come?" Brother smiling all over hisself.

"Couldn't help but know. You done mentioned it more times than a little." Mama give Brother some syrup and biscuits. Then she fix me some too.

I pull the top off my biscuit and dab it in some syrup. "You not eating none, Mama?"

"I done ate already, with your daddy," Mama tells me. But she set down anyway. "That reminds me. Your daddy want you and Brother to gather up your clothes." Now I see a grin in her eyes. And I know she fixing to tell us something good. So I just play like I ain't caught on yet.

"Why we hafta gather up our clothes for?"

" 'Cause your daddy done got word from Jamie, and he s'pose to come and take y'all for a while. And he mentioned something about possum hunting."

I almost hop clean up from the table. "For true?" I says to Mama, like I ain't heard straight the first time. "Granddaddy's coming? You mean me and Brother, we going to Grandma's house? And we going possum hunting along wit it?"

Mama nods her head. And I feel my grin stretching until it nearly about reach my ears.

"Hot dog! Granddaddy's coming and the rolling store too!" Brother jump up and start flapping his arms like chicken wings. "Boy oh boy! We gonna have us a good ole time!"

"And I got another surprise in store for y'all when you come back."

"Another surprise?" I says. "What kind it gonna be?"

"I'm not gon' say another word about it." Mama got a grin in her eyes again. "Y'all just have to wait and see."

"Hot dog!" Brother keep jitterbugging round until Mama make him set down before his biscuits be stone cold. "I betcha when Granddaddy come he gon' be in his Chevrolet. And I gonna set by the door." Brother wipe his mouth on the dish rag.

"Who said you could?"

"My ownself."

"Well, you ain't. I is."

Brother trails me out back to slop the hogs. Still running his mouth.

"But I said it first."

"Makes no difference. I'm the oldest."

"You not the oldest. Doris is."

"She don't count none. She just a half-sister."

Brother frown up his face at me. "Mama done told you 'bout calling our other sisters half ones. And when they come here, she say you better not be cutting up, like you done before. Else she gonna give you a good whipping."

"What you know about it?" I says right quick. "You don't even know what happened. It was all Maybaby's fault." I cock my head to one side and screw my face up, remembering Maybaby telling her big fat stories. She knowed good and well I never said nothing about us not having room for them. I just told her that they better go someplace and make them a family, 'cause ours already filled up.

"Shoot," I say to Brother. "It's not my fault they daddy didn't marry Mama and our daddy did. Maybaby just trying to hold it against me. That's all. Wit her ole mean self. If it was up to me, all three of them could stay wit Great-Grandma Moriah until the cows come home. And that goes double for Maybaby. I hope our surprise is all over before she come. So she won't be in on it. And I hope this summer goes faster than anything, so's they can go on back where they come from."

"Annie Rye, you better quit talking bad 'bout our sisters."

"They ain't my sisters. None of 'em. Not Doris. Not Brat. And *not* Maybaby. And you better hush your mouth, before I tell Daddy you been sucking up your lip."

Right quick Brother loosens his bottom lip from under his top one. "If I don't set 'side the door, I'm not gonna swap none of my stuff witcha when the rolling store comes."

Me and Brother didn't have no time to map out who was going to set next to the door, 'cause before we make it to the hogpen, Miz Soota start rubbing her head on the fence post, just a-grunting. All the other hogs rooting in the mud and going on. Just slowpoking around. Not Miz Soota. She come right off. She can smell good slop a mile away.

"Miz Soota," I says, emptying the bucket, "you mean to tell me you still in this here pen? You don't plan on busting out today?"

Brother hop up on the fence and lean over Miz Soota's head. "Why you not eating up Mama's watermelons?"

"Don't you pay Brother no mind, Miz Soota. He just poking fun at you 'cause he can't eat none. Anyways, Daddy thinks the sun rise and sets in you. Mama says so."

"And Mama says you more trouble than you worth," Brother puts in.

"For true, Miz Soota? Is that for true?"

Miz Soota grunts. And me and Brother start laughing and saying our saying.

> *"Bring out the sugar*
> *And bring out the tea—*
> *Miz Soota, Miz Soota,*
> *The blackest hog I ever did see—*
> *Black as soot in the chimney."*

Brother jump down off the fence like he always do. "Bet I can beatcha back to the house."

Soon as he have a lead, I grab up the slop buckets and take off behind him. Sometime I let him win, like I'm doing now. Else he might start falling out and acting like a big baby. And it'll take us forever to git our work did.

"I'm the champeen, ain't I, Annie Rye? Ain't I?"

"Yep. You the champeen. Now we best git done wit our work. You go feed the chickens, while I sweep the yard. The rolling store liable to come anytime now."

Brother don't waste no time. He take off real quick. And I start sweeping the yard with dog fenders, some long, skinny branches Mama done tied together with old rags. But I be knowing he liable to be right back any minute being worrisome. And sho nuff. Before I turn around good, Brother come jerking on my clothes.

"Annie Rye, look."

When I gaze towards the dirt road where Brother pointing at, I see this little teen-ouncy girl walking up to the house. Don't look to be old as Brother. And she white. Time she spot us watching, she stop at the edge of the yard, swinging her arms. Before long she done inched all the way where me and Brother standing at.

It sho seem strange. Her wandering around all

by herself. I glance up the long stretch of road and back. Not a single soul in sight. There's no other houses setting along this road. Except for the Giffords, and they not even in hollering distance. Anyways, they colored. So I can't figure out where she done come from. Seeing how don't too many white folks live hereabouts. Must be another sharecropper done moved in.

"Where you stay at?" I ask, noticing the patched-up sack dress she got on.

At first she don't say nothing. Just rock on the back part of her feet. After a while, she point out by the pecan orchard.

"Over yonder."

Then she hush and just stand there doing like before. Just rocking on the back part of her feet. And before I can figure out what she up to, she done walked right by me and Brother and done took her a seat on the front porch. Setting there dangling her legs over the side. Just making herself right at home.

Now Brother go take him a seat too. "Whatcha doing over here? You looking for somebody?"

She still won't say much of nothing. Just push her shoulders up and keep staring out across the yard, swinging her feet. Brother swing his too.

"Whatcha name?"

"Sissy."

"My name Buddy Boy."

"Brother, your name not no Buddy Boy," I put in.

"But that's what Miz Hattie Bell call me. And she call Elouise Moochie Gal."

"I know, but Miz Hattie Bell just be funnying you. So you stop telling people that."

"Yeah," Brother says, turning back to Sissy, "Buddy Boy just my made-up name. Not my real name. Ira Lee Footman, Junior. That's my real one. Right, Annie Rye?"

Before I can answer Brother back, he talking about something else.

"You wanna come in the house and see my playthings?" I overhear Brother saying when I go back to sweeping the yard.

"Brother," I hollers at him. "You can't be taking no . . . I mean, Elouise sleep, and y'all might wake her up."

I'm halfway watching Brother and her on the porch and halfway sweeping the yard. 'Cause if something was to happen to that little white girl while she was here at our house, we'd never hear the last of it. So I knows I'd better keep my eye on her and maybe pretty soon somebody'll come hunting to see where she at.

Brother don't hardly have nobody his own age to play with. So he just as glad as he can be. I can tell 'cause he running his mouth like crazy.

"Elouise always stay in the house where Mama at. 'Cause she can't walk. She too little."

"I don't got no mama."

"You ain't got no mama? Where she at?"

Sissy hunch her shoulders up. "I dunno."

"Then you can come over here and my mama can see after you. Then you can have a mama just like me. OK?"

" 'K." Sissy fold her arms across a head full of straggly hair that look just like a penny. All rusty red. And I could tell she not use to being around no colored folk, 'cause now she steady trying to rub the dark off Brother's skin. But Brother, he not paying that no attention. He just says, "We got us a bald-head chicken round on the back," and jump off the porch, grinning. Sissy mock Brother, doing like he do. Brother rear back and prop his hands on his sides.

> *"Baldy-scaldy,*
> *Nineteen-forty,*
> *Kiss my gal*
> *And call me Shorty.*

"That's what that ole chicken say. Wanna go see?"

Sissy smother her grin with one hand and grab Brother's with her other one.

I stand the yard broom up against the house and follow behind Brother and Sissy, mumbling to myself. "Shoot. How's I'm s'pose to git on wit my work? Folk oughta keep up wit they own chillun. Ain't my duty to be doing it for 'em. And don't even seem like nobody even coming." The words barely out of my mouth good before somebody hollering after us.

When I turn towards the road, a tall, bony white boy standing by the fence post. His face steaming red. He mad as all git-up.

"Where you taking Sissy? Leave her be. Sissy, git over here."

Sissy drop Brother's hand and run across the yard. " 'K, J.D."

"And y'all keep your paws to yourself." J.D. wag his finger at me.

"Nobody ain't done nothing to her. We ain't had no notion where she come from. So we let her stay until somebody come looking."

"Got no need for none a your help." J.D. eye me and Brother up and down, sucking his teeth. Then he snap at Sissy. "And why ya gotta always go wandering off for? Pa gonna tan your hide good. Now git." J.D. boot Sissy with his foot, and she take off across the road. "Got no business wit nobody like them noways."

J.D. never once set foot in our yard. He act like we was poison or something. I didn't like the looks of J.D. Not because he was white or nothing. He just didn't set right with me. I could tell he had a mean streak in him a mile wide. And I knowed, too, we'd better be on the lookout. He was bound to be nothing but natural-born trouble.

Me and Brother watch as they disappear amongst the pecan trees. Then Brother start pulling on his lip, looking all pitiful.

"Come on, Brother. You not s'pose to be playing wit no white chillun nohow."

"Why, Annie Rye?"

" 'Cause. Just 'cause. That's all. Now gon' and watch for the rolling store, so's you can git some jawbone breakers."

Now that Brother out the way, it don't take no time to git the yard did. And soon as I go put the yard broom beneath the front porch, I hear Brother hollering like crazy. So I pat on my pocket, to see if my pennies still in there, 'cause I knows the rolling store is coming. I hollers for Mama. And she come out the house, toting Elouise on her hip.

Now I see a big red buslike contraption coming down the road and pulling up right out front—horn beeping and the chicken coop underneath just swinging. Brother hopping around real crazy. Acting like he having a fit or something. Mama tells him to be still, but it don't do no good. 'Cause he go to jumping up all over again when the white man open the back door and put down some wooden steps.

"Whee-ooo," the man says to Mama, when all us

climb inside. "Ain't it hot today, and drier than a Georgia pine."

But me and Brother not thinking about no Georgia pine. We trying to see all what he got in there. On both sides where the shelves at, chicken wire nailed up, so's the goods won't fall while the store going from place to place. And he got plenty too. I betcha this about the best rolling store in all Decatur County. It carries just about anything you could think up. There's even rice in a big barrel that you dip up with a little silver dipper. And more than that. There's all sorts of good stuff. That's what I got my mind on. On the good stuff. And I see some in great big jars setting in wood slots on the counter. I slide my hands across the slick glass. Next to one is wrote "2 for 1¢." It's all stacked full with sugar cookies. Another got red and black licorice setting in it. Then one got peppermint sticks all the way to the brim.

"Mmm-umph!" Brother poke me with his elbow. "Lookit all them jawbone breakers!"

"Yeah, and all them sugar cookies sho do make my mouth water," I says, shifting my eyes over at all them soda waters: RC, Pepsi-Cola, and chocolate too. I start licking my lips.

"What you gonna git, Annie Rye?" Brother says in a low voice.

"I ain't made up my mind yet."

I'm squeezing sawdust between my toes and

smelling King Edward cigars, the kind Grand-daddy smokes, when Mama says, "Annie Rye, did you hear me? What y'all gon' buy?"

I hunch up my shoulders and let them fall back down. Mama turns back to the man. "Let me have a sack of that flour. If I can save a few more of them flower prints, I can sew up Annie Rye a real nice dress." Mama studies the flour sack some. "Now what y'all want?"

"I didn't figure it out yet."

"Well, this man don't have all day."

"I want some of them jawbone breakers." Brother speaks up right quick and hand the man his pennies.

My eyes go from the chewing gum to the cookies to the Mary Janes and back to the chewing gum again.

"I want some of them peppermint sticks."

Time the man have the jar unscrewed, I cut my eyes back down the counter.

"I changed my mind. I want some Mary Janes."

"Annie Rye . . ." Mama looks at me sideways, and I knowed I better not change my mind another time. So I reach in my pocket and unloosen the pennies in my rag.

Soon as we all done buying our stuff, the rolling store heads on down the road. Mama and Elouise go on back in the house. And me and Brother set underneath the black walnut tree, laughing and

sucking jawbone breakers and chewing Mary Janes
and saying our little saying:

> *"Yo' eyes may shine,*
> *Yo' teeth may grit—*
> *But none a this*
> *You'll never git."*

I swallow the last of my Mary Jane. "You wanna
do some chunking, Brother?" I pick up a dried-out
walnut and spatters dirt across the road.

"Naw. I gotta go use it."

Before I can say another word, Brother halfway
across the field to the outhouse. No use waiting on
him neither. No telling when he gon' be back. So I
aim me a walnut across the road again, and I hears
whistling. And I knowed it was my daddy, coming
back from tending the turkeys up at ole man Myszell's place. He the man Daddy do sharecropping
with. I run to meet up with him, and he hoist me
on his shoulders.

"Gal, you gitting too big for me to be toting you
like this."

"Naw I ain't, Daddy," I says, hanging on to his
neck. "Anyways, yesterday you said I was skinny
as a pond guinea."

Daddy laugh real hard. And I do too.

"Know what, Daddy? I been working on my
chunking. And my dip-see-do you done showed me,

coming 'long real good. I crooked my knees just a pinch and burst that dirt wide open. Pretty soon I'm gonna be able to be a baseball thrower just like you is."

"If I don't watch out, they'll have you pitching for the Boweevils insteada me."

"Ahh, Daddy, you just spoofing me."

Daddy laugh again.

"Whatcha ma been doing?" That's the name he said for Mama and what he called his mama too. "Ma."

"She fixing some supper. You hungry, Daddy?"

Before he can answer me back, Brother come running from around the house. "I wanna be up there too," he says, pulling on Daddy's britches.

So Daddy let me down and hoist Brother up, same as me. My daddy is about the tallest man I ever saw, so Brother setting up real high. And Daddy ride him all the way to the front porch and set him down.

"Who you gonna pick up next?" Brother says. But Daddy don't give him no answer, 'cause he already gone in the door. Now Elouise start giggling, and we know she having a chance too. Me and Brother start skipping around the yard, acting crazy and giggling. Even when rain go to dropping on our head, it don't bother us none. We just keep on twisting our feet and wiggling our arms and singing:

> *"Do the hucka buck,*
> *Wobble like a duck—*
> *That's the way you do*
> *When you do the hucka buck."*

Me and Brother is having ourselves a good time, popping our fingers and going on. Then I see Mama come out on the porch, and I know we in big trouble.

chapter 2

June Bugs and Crackling Bread

>>>>>>>>>>>>>>>>>>>>>>>>>>>>>>>>>

"I'M GON' WOBBLE your duck." Mama prop
her hands on her hips. "Git in here. Just look at
y'all. Playing in this rain, cool as it is. Y'all know
better than this."

Me and Brother quit our dancing and climb up
the steps right quick. We don't say nary word. We
just try to sneak past Mama. But she catches Brother's ear. And mines too.

"Ooow! That hurt." I try slipping on in the house,
but Mama catch hold to my sleeve.

"It s'pose to hurt."

Brother can't say "Ooow," 'cause he sneezing too
much.

"Just listen at Brother, and he just gitting over a
cold. And you liable to be next, Annie Rye." Mama

give me and Brother another ear pulling. "If y'all got any more notions of gitting in devilment, y'all won't be going nary step when Jamie gits here. Mark my words. Just watch what I say."

Mama meant every word she done said. And she had her eye on me and Brother the whole time. Right up until Granddaddy pulled up in the yard.

"Granddaddy," I says, opening up the car on his side. "What done took you so long?"

"Yeah, Granddaddy." Brother jump off the porch and come where Granddaddy standing at. "What done took you so long?"

"Daddy say it's not but twenty miles betwixt here and Amsterdam," I tell him when he bend down so's I can hug his neck. "Just a hop, skip, and a jump."

"Aw, ain't took that long. No such thing," he says, with his King Edward cigar caught between his teeth.

"Umm-huh, Granddaddy." Brother bob his head and catch him by the leg. Granddaddy try to shake him loose, but Brother still hang on. So Granddaddy tickle him in the side.

"Watch out now, Jitterbug."

Brother start giggling and fall back on the ground. "You not playing fair, Granddaddy. You ain't s'pose to outdo me. I had you first."

Granddaddy was fixing to grab Brother again, when Mama come out on the porch with Elouise.

"Jamie, I got biscuits warming on the stove. Come on in so I can set you a plate."

"Naw, Mit," he tell Mama, scratching his bald spot. "I best be heading on back. Already way over in the evening."

Then me and Brother put our bundles in the back and climb in the front seat with Granddaddy and head towards Amsterdam. And I could tell Brother glad, 'cause he keep on inching around in the seat and asking a whole bunch of questions and saying "holy smokes." But Granddaddy don't mind none much. He just roll his King Edward cigar around in his mouth and says, "If I let ya in on all the answers, pretty soon you'd be smarter than me." Granddaddy wink his eye at me. And I wink right back. I knowed he was just funning with Brother. Now it don't matter none much who set beside the door. So first Brother take him a turn. Then I take me one. And it don't matter none at all. Me and Brother just glad we on our way to Grandma's house, riding in Granddaddy's Chevrolet.

Brother done run his mouth so much, he done wore hisself out. Now he over there sleeping next to Granddaddy. Not me. Shoot no. I can't be missing nothing. I set up straight and rub my eyeballs. Soon I hears barking, and I know it must be ole Duke and Trixy. So I raise up off the seat. And sho nuff, Granddaddy's bloodhounds crawling from underneath the front porch. Then I see somebody

light-skinned peeping out the window. And I know
it's Grandma.

I poke Brother on the knee. "Wake up. We at
Grandma's house."

"We is?" I hear Brother say. But I don't answer
him back, 'cause I'm already climbing up the steps.

"Well, looka here," Grandma says, stretching out
her arms and hugging me real tight.

"Gal, you growing straight up. Just like a bean-
pole. When you gon' put some meat on them bones?"

"I dunno, Grandma."

She laugh and give me another squeeze. "Where
Brother at?" Grandma let me loose and fix her head
rag.

"Here I is. Down here."

"Well, you just bring yo'self up here and give yo'
Grandma some sugar."

Brother go to hanging back, picking at his lip.
Acting all shamefaced.

"Ah, go on, Brother. Stop trying to act like a
baby. Grandma not gonna bitecha."

Brother inch his way up to where Grandma's at,
and she hug him same as me.

"If ya ain't the spitting image of yo' uncle Charlie
Clark, I'd pay anybody."

I knowed Grandma would say that. 'Cause she
do it every time we come over here.

"Yes sir, the spitting image." Grandma straighten
her back up. "Now y'all come on in the house so

Grandma can fix y'all something. Jamie," Grandma says to Granddaddy, "you wanna bite to eat?"

Granddaddy still setting halfway in the car. "Not now, Annie. Think I'll set a spell." Granddaddy's voice had a funny squeak in it.

"That leg worrying you, ain't it, Jamie?"

" 'Taint nothing, woman. Now y'all gon' in the house, and I'll be on directly."

So me and Brother go on in the house and watch while Grandma rake sweet 'tatoes out the fireplace.

"Hand me some tin plates, so's I can give y'all some of these here 'tatoes." Grandma point at the shelf in back of her. And me and Brother don't waste no time neither. When I see Grandma uncover a big fat 'tato from beneath the ashes, I start to stick my plate out, and Brother jump in front of me.

"I want that one."

"Stop being a greedy gut," I holler at him.

"Now. Now. No need kicking up a fuss. There's plenty." Grandma drop a 'tato in Brother's tin plate. Then she gives me a big one same as him and go back to raking more 'tatoes out.

"Now watch out, so's y'all don't git ya tongue burned. Let them 'tatoes cool a bit."

But me and Brother already peeling the hull off and splitting our 'tatoes down the middle.

Granddaddy comes in the house, limping worse than he did before. A tractor turned over on him when he was a young man. Broke his leg clean in two. Never did grown back right, Grandma says, 'cause Granddaddy wouldn't be still and do like he was s'pose to. Now one leg shorter than the other one.

I figures his leg must be bothering him pretty bad. So I says, "Granddaddy, you set down and I'll bring your liniment."

"Well, I reckon it is worrying me a pinch. Must be this cool spell we been having." He cut his eyes over at Grandma. She don't say nary word, just pull down on her head rag and keep on raking in the ashes.

"Grandma," I says, handing Granddaddy his medicine, "where Goudi and them at?"

"They over at Shorty's house. And since the sun done gone down, I don't spect they'll be making it back till in the morning sometime. So you hafta sleep in Goudi's bed by yo'self."

Uncle Shorty is Grandma's oldest youngun and Goudi is the youngest one. But Grandma got lots more besides them. Uncle Junior. Uncle Robert. Then come Uncle Leroy and . . .

"Annie Rye," I hear Grandma say, "you listening at me? Finish eating yo' 'tato 'fore it git cold."

"Yes'm, Grandma. I will."

"Grandma, can old Duke and Trixy . . ." Brother didn't have a chance to finish out his words, 'cause he go to coughing.

"Cover your mouth up, boy!" I stretch my hands

over my plate. "Don't be spreading your germs over my food!"

"Now, Annie Rye, don't be so hard on yo' brother."

"But he knows better, Grandma. Mama done told him eleven dozen times to turn his head when he got to cough, so's he won't be coughing all over people."

"Sometimes it takes some of us a little longer to come up to where we oughta be. And maybe some of us never will. The good Lord ain't made none a us perfect. We all got our shortcomings. That's why we gotta take a little and give a little. And bear along wit each other. Make allowances." Grandma strike a match and light the kerosene lamp. "That's what being a family is all about."

"Yes'm, Grandma." I hang my head down.

"None a that now. You just bring yo'self on over here and give yo' Grandma some sugar."

I drag over where Grandma at, and she gives me a good squeezing. "Now that's more like it. Grandma still love her gal. Even if she do look like a knock-kneed pond guinea."

"Ah, Grandma, you sound just like Daddy." Me and her go to laughing. And Grandma gives me another squeezing, and I squeeze her right back.

Brother start hanging on Grandma's apron. So she let me loose so's she can pay attention to him.

"Can I? Huh, Grandma? Can ole Duke and Trixy sleep wit me? Huh?"

"I s'pose it ain't gon' hurt nothing. You can have a pallet here 'side the fireplace."

"Hot dog! H-e-r-e, Duke. Come on, boy."

Duke come crawling out the corner and lick on Brother. Trixy do too.

Grandma got one of her quilts so's she can fix Brother a pallet to lay on. Before she can spread it out good, Brother setting on it with Duke's head in his lap.

"You gonna tell us one of them stories back when you was just knee high to a grasshopper? Huh, Granddaddy?"

I set down on the floor next to Granddaddy's chair. "One about what happened back in the olden days. A scary one. Real scary."

Granddaddy roll his cigar around in his mouth like he always do when he thinking on what he fixing to say. Then he starts off. "When I was coming up, we all stayed just in hollering distance of Timber Creek. Down near Coon Hollow. Back then there weren't no regular doctors going round like nowadays. So the curing was mainly up to Ma Clark. So she kept a right smart of roots and herbs on hand. Well, come to find out she had run low on roots one day and wanted me to fetch some. The first thing you know, yo' uncle Charlie spouting off at the mouth. Saying how he hoped I didn't hafta go traipsing round in Coon Hollow.

"Now, he knowed good and well Coon Hollow was the only place Ma Clark's roots growed at. And he knowed, too, how spooky it could be down in the hollow. And he just come straight out and say, 'Mean to tell me you ain't heard? Well, maybe it ain't much to mention. And maybe I ought not say, seeing how you hafta go down in them woods all by yo'self. But talk has it ole Sam Turner roaming round in them woods somewhere.' Then Charlie go on to say how talk had it ole Sam weren't right in the head. And how he had gone mad and run off to Coon Hollow. And how if he was to catch you, he'd make you eat green liver and snake eyes. Then leave you to puke yo' guts out. But if you was to be carrying a dried chicken foot or two, ole Sam might take a notion to let ya slip loose. Seeing how he was partial to 'em.

"Ma Clark said it was just a tale. Not a stitch of truth to it. Now, I shoulda figured as much, seeing how Charlie had a way of stretching the truth and given to pulling pranks and the like. So I weren't putting much stock in nothing he done said. But I weren't taking Ma Clark's word just like that neither. I stuffed my pockets full of green chinaberries and got my slingshot. Then me and Li'l Bit head down in Coon Hollow. Li'l Bit was my dog. No size to 'er. But she weren't feared of nothing. Dead or live."

"Just like ole Duke," Brother holler out. "He ain't afeared of nothing neither. Is you, boy?"

"S-s-sh." I frown at him. "Now," I says, turning back to Granddaddy, "what happen next?"

Granddaddy lean forward in his straight chair and spit in the fire. "Well sir, I had just got done digging the last of Ma Clark's roots and put 'em in my sack, when something or the other come crawling out the bushes on all fours. My throat got dry as corn shucks. The critter started to rear up. Move towards me. Right then I grabbed my slingshot and let him have it wit them chinaberries. Li'l Bit lit into him, and he hightailed it back in the bushes. And me and Li'l Bit, we struck out towards the house. Partway, it come to mind that weren't nobody but Charlie, up to his tomfoolery agin. But he'd think twice from now on. Li'l Bit got him good. Nabbed him right in the seat of his britches. And I knowed he wouldn't be setting down for a week.

"Me and Li'l Bit took the shortcut home so's I could beat Charlie to the house and have a good laugh when he hobbled in. Well sir, I opened the door, and there set Charlie. Pretty as you please. Ma Clark had lanced the boil on his heel. Charlie hadn't set foot out the house all day.

"From then on, I made sho I had a dried chicken

foot or two on me whenever I'd hafta make a trip down in Coon Hollow."

Granddaddy make little shivers run down my back the way he said H-o-l-l-o-w, and I inch up closer to his chair. "Did you ever find out what was out there?"

"Never did. Naw sir. Still blaffs me some. But I reckon it coulda been my mind playing tricks on me. Them woods being so dark and all. But then agin"—Granddaddy don't crack a smile—"it coulda been ole Sam."

My eyes stretch big as saucers. "Brother," I says right quick, "I'm gonna take Trixy in here where I'm sleeping at so's you and ole Duke can have more room on your pallet." I hop in Goudi's bed and cover my head up and don't take it out no more until I hear Goudi telling me it's daylight and time for me to git up so's I can help fetch Grandma some spring water.

Me and Goudi go on down in the woods, with ole Duke trailing behind. Goudi is Grandma's girl. She got two more besides her. Munch and Sister. They the biggest ones. And they all my daddy's sisters. All my aunties. Goudi is too. But she don't seem like it, 'cause I nearly as old as her.

The spring a good piece back in the woods. Me and Goudi run part the way with ole Duke, so it don't take us that long. But we got to take our time on the way back 'cause our tin buckets filled up to the rim with cold water. And they heavy some. But Goudi don't set her two down. So I don't neither. We just tote them on to the house like there's nothing to it.

Grandma keep great big barrels in the kitchen for holding water. And soon as we empty our buckets out, she tell us to run along and busy ourselves doing something else. So me and Goudi go on the porch and hang our legs over the side.

"What kinda devilment Brat and them been gitting into?" Goudi ask right off.

I twist my mouth to one side. Why Goudi have to go and bring them up for? It's bad enough they coming to stay with us for the summer. And I'm sho not gon' be thinking about them while I'm here at Grandma's, 'cause I know by the time I'm back home good they'll be popping up. Shoot. They been with Great-Grandma Moriah since before I can remember. And she got plenty of room for them. Not like at our house. I can't even much breathe unless one of them up in my face. So it don't make no sense for them to visit us at all. Not even every once in a while like they been doing. And the more I thinks on it, the madder I git. Red-hot mad. So mad I hardly know it when Goudi hunch me in the side.

"Annie Rye? What Brat and them been doing?"

I felt just like saying, "If you wanna know so

much about 'em, go find out for yourself. I ain't no telegraph lady." But I just says, as mannerly as I can, "I don't see 'em that much." Just so Goudi will hush about them. But she go right on running her mouth.

"I bet you miss 'em, don'tcha?"

"Don't bother me none."

Goudi stop swinging her feet. "Girl, you mean to tell me them your sisters and you not missing 'em? Huh. Bet if it was me, I sho would."

"You just saying that 'cause you like to be round Brat. Anyways, they just half-sisters. Not real ones."

"Annie Rye, you gonna git it for real this time. Mama done told you 'bout calling them half-sisters." A smarty-pants voice comes up through the boards.

"Brother, you stop eavesdropping on my conversation. Come on from under that house."

Me and Goudi jump down where Brother standing at. "I ain't eavesdropping. I was just listening at what y'all talking 'bout."

I shake my finger in his face. "Well, next time stop up your ears."

Now ole Duke and Trixy crawls out, stretching against Brother's legs.

"Anyhow," I says, "why don't you go play wit somebody your own size? Like Duke and Trixy."

"I don't wanna play with Granddaddy's hound dogs no more. I wanna follow y'all."

"We plan on catching us some June bugs. Right?"

I look at Goudi real quick and keep on talking to Brother. "And we don't want you scaring 'em off." Brother come trailing behind me and Goudi.

"I won't scare 'em. I just wanna catch me some too."

I draw in my breath and blow it out hard. "OK. You can come. But don't go keeping up too much noise."

Brother says he promise. But I'm not believing a word he says, 'cause he always running his mouth. And sho nuff, time we walk out in the field, Brother starts hollering all over the place soon as we find one.

"See there, Brother. Look what you done." I prop my hands on my hips. "You done made us lose that June bug."

"Naw I didn't neither. He just fell off in them weeds all by hisself. He must be got the heebie-jeebies. I bet I find me some bigger than that."

And sho as gravy, he done got three bugs, one right after the other. Big ones too. Now we all got us a fat June bug. And we tie some string around their back legs and chunk them up in the air. It didn't take them no time to git worn out. Flying all them zigzags and everything. So we turn them back loose.

We could tell Grandma's cooking up some good stuff, 'cause it's smelling all the way outside. So I walk around back, high up on some can walkers

Goudi done made out of pork 'n' bean cans, and see if I can peep in the window.

"Grandma, the food ready yet?"

"Naw it ain't," I hear her say.

"Grandma."

"Whatcha want now, gal?"

"Grandma, I wanna eat."

"Me too, Grandma." Brother come up behind me.

Grandma lean out the door. She got her head all wrapped up like they used to do in the olden days. "If y'all younguns ain't got a notion to wait till I done, then come on and git some a this here ration."

Before Grandma got her words out good, me and Brother in the back door. Grandma done already fried up some crackling bread. She cut me and Brother some great big hunks.

My grandma knowed how to cook better than anybody in all Decatur County. 'Specially that possum Granddaddy done caught night before last. I smell it cooking in hot sauce. And I knows it got sweet 'tatoes laying alongside. So I ease on up to Grandma. She don't pay me no mind. She just keeps stirring in her collard green pot. So I stick my hand in her apron pocket. Then I gaze straight at her, "begging wit my eyes." That's what Grandma calls it. She don't mind none though. She smiles like she always do, and I feel all warm inside, just like she was covering me up in one of her big quilts.

chapter 3

Double Pneumonia

>>>>>>>>>>>>>>>>>>>>>>>>>>>>>>>>>>>

SOME DAYS LATER, we all set to go possum hunting like Granddaddy done promised, when Brother start coughing and puking up. Grandma got that funny look on her face, and I know what she fixing to say. So I tell her Brother not sick or nothing, he just done eat more than his belly can hold. Now he done throwed up some, he liable to be feeling better. But Grandma's not taking my word or nothing. She makes Brother go lay down. And she says if he no better off before the sun finish going down, we won't be going nary step. 'Specially no possum hunting.

Come next morning, I just knowed Brother would be up and doing like he always do. And sho nuff. I sees him setting on his side of the bed, petting on ole Duke. So I tell him don't be tiring ole Duke out, 'cause we going possum hunting come nightfall. Brother don't say nothing. He just start coughing his head off and puking up again. I guess that means we not going possum hunting—we going right back home. All on account of Brother.

I try to tell Grandma I'm not the one sick. Brother is. So I oughta have a chance to stay. But she and Granddaddy go ahead and bring me on back home along with Brother.

Granddaddy promised he would come after us when Brother got over his puking and everything. But that's not liable to be until doomsday, 'cause Brother coughing harder now than he did before. Not even Grandma's root tonic do no good. And Granddaddy says it oughta cure a mule. But not Brother. He keeps right on coughing and breathing like he got a whistle hung up in his throat. Mama says the cold done settle down in his chest. And she can't figure out how to loosen it up. So Daddy decided Dr. Maxwell oughta look at him. And more than likely, they won't be back before nightfall. So I brung in some logs, so's me and Elouise has a fire going. Mama says she was liable to be fretful, seeing how she cutting some pegs. But Elouise didn't worry me none. She mostly just catnapping. And she still about half asleep when I hear Daddy's car pull in the yard. So I ease her back down on her pallet and unlatch the door.

"How's Brother?"

"Same as before" is all Daddy says, and walks on by me with Brother, wrapped up in bedcovers.

But I knowed Brother was worse off than I thought, 'cause Mama looking down at the floor. "Brother done got pneumonia," she says.

THAT WAS two weeks ago. Brother still got a fever, even after he done took all that gooey-looking medicine Dr. Maxwell gave him. And his lips all parched up and his eyes white as cotton. All he do is lay curled in Mama's bed. He won't eat nothing much, so Mama just feed him pot liquor. Mr. Myszell told her Brother apt to git worse before he git better. So he sent for Dr. Maxwell to come out to the house. Grandma and Granddaddy come back too.

I can tell Daddy sho is worried up a good fashion. He ain't been saying much of nothing—just standing alongside Granddaddy, with his elbow on top of the mantelpiece and looking at the fire. Grandma here too—on the set-tee next to me. She holding her arms and steady rocking. All you can hear is the fire crackling and that ole owl hooting outside in the dark. I start having that scary feeling down in my belly. Just like a mudfish wallowing around.

After a while, Dr. Maxwell come out the room where Brother's at. "He's a mighty sick boy."

"I knowed that much before you come," Daddy snap at Dr. Maxwell. "Now what can be did?"

I set straight up, my eyes bucking. Daddy don't mostly speak that way to nobody. 'Specially no white folks. But Dr. Maxwell don't seem like he mad none. He just looks at Daddy and says, "I know you're concerned about your youngun. But there ain't nothing else I can do. He's got double pneumonia." Then he looks at Mama. "Mit, keep him bathed in rubbing alcohol. If we break the fever, there be a good chance he'll pull through. I'll be up at Myszell's place for a spell, if there be any change."

Double pneumonia. The best I could make out was Brother done got another pneumonia on top of the one he had the first time. And I guess that was about the worse kind you could have.

Granddaddy roll his cigar around in his mouth and chunk some wood on the fire. All the time that funny kind of quiet is creeping up. Like all us holding our breath and don't remember how to let it loose. I can't figure out what to do with myself. I just know I can't set here in this same spot no more. So I peep in the kitchen, where I seen Mama go. And I see her looking up at the loft, praying.

"Lord, you knows all 'bout these troubles of mine. So I ain't gon' be taking up mucha your time. My youngun in there low sick. The doctor done give him up. He yourn, Lord. You got every hair on his head numbered. So if you could just find it in your goodness . . . Oh, Lord . . . please won'tcha spare my child."

Now that ole mudfish is out my belly and balled up in my throat, pushing water out my eyes. And I hears that hooting owl. "Who-o-o who-o-o."

I ease back on the set-tee. Next thing I know, just a little peep of light slipping betwixt the curtains and the rooster crowing. And I know morning done already come. So I tiptoe in where Brother laying down. He sho don't look right, laying there all stretched out with his eyes shut. I move up close, next to the bed. "When you all well, Brother, I promise to shoot marbles wit you whenever you want to. And I gonna let you play wit my tea set too." Brother don't move nary inch. "You remember the rolling store's coming. Don'tcha wanna meet the rolling store and git some of them jawbone breakers?"

Brother don't say nothing back. He just lay there all stiff like, and his eyes don't even open up. So I feel on his head to see how his fever doing. And there was that ole mudfish again messing with me. And while I'm trying to swallow down that balled-up feeling in my throat, I hear somebody saying, "What's wrong wit you, Annie Rye?" And Brother's looking right at me.

"Ain't nothing wrong wit me," I say right quick. "I just got something in my eye, that's all."

Next thing I know, Daddy and them is all crowded around where Brother's at.

"How ya feeling, Jitterbug?" Granddaddy ask right off.

And Brother don't waste no time letting him know. "Like I wanna eat."

All us bust out laughing. Now I knows for sho Brother was gon' be out that bed in no time. 'Cause he done got his mind dead set on putting something in his belly.

chapter 4

Half-Sisters

>>>>>>>>>>>>>>>>>>>>>>>>>>>>>>>>>>>

IT BEEN some time since Brother was low sick. But Mama say he not out the woods yet. More than likely that's why she didn't mention nothing about the surprise she been saving up for me and him. But I sho hope she hurry up and make haste about it, 'cause she say Brat and them s'pose to be coming later on this week. That's worse than that pneumonia she say can jump back on you if you don't watch out. So Mama not letting Brother be ripping and running loose. That's why he still in the house and I'm out here all by myself, chunking at them pecan trees setting across the road. And I just fixing to take me another good aim, when I catch sight of Daddy's car coming toward the house. And I just know my eyes fooling me. That can't be them.

My mouth drop wide open. They ain't s'pose to be here yet. But it's them all right. I see them plain as day. 'Cause somebody got they head hanging out the window. I run back to the porch and stomp my foot, stomp it hard as I can.

"Shoot. Ahhh, shoot."

"What's ailing you, keeping up all that racket?" Mama got her head sticking out the door. "If you wake Elouise up, you gon' tend to her."

"Daddy done brung a whole carload of chillun home wit him."

"I figured he'd be pulling in here directly." Mama comes on out the door. "Left before daylight this morning, on his way to Moriah's to pick them up."

"Nobody never told me today was when they s'pose to be here." I prop myself up against a post and mumbles under my breath. "I don't see why they hafta come here at all."

"Annie Rye, don't go acting like that. Them your sisters. And you knowed they was gon' come."

I twist my mouth to one side. "Yes'm, Mama. I know. But I didn't think it would be this quick. And I still—"

"Annie Rye." Mama cut me off. "This just couldn't be helped. Your daddy just found out late last night that Mr. Myszell had some more work for him to do later on this week, so he had to take off this morning. This was the only time he could leave. And I didn't have a chance to tell y'all this morning yet." Mama take me by the shoulders. "Now go in the house and see if Elouise done woke up. And you mind your manners, you hear?"

Mama got that "I ain't having no more of you back talk" look on her face, so I go on in the house like I been told.

She always talking about it makes no difference that I'Lee not they real daddy. She says all us come out of her, and that makes us just plain sisters. Huh! I don't care what nobody say, they still just half-sisters. Not whole ones. Not like me and Brother and Elouise.

"What's ail you, Annie Rye? Mama got at you 'bout something?" Brother have to know, time I walk in the door.

"Yeah. And it's all they fault."

"Who you talking 'bout?"

"You know, them other girls. Them that stay wit Great-Grandma Moriah."

I push my mouth out far as it can go. "Daddy done brung 'em back and they not even s'pose to be here yet."

"Ooh. You mean our other sisters. Hot dog!"

"They ain't my sisters. They just half-sisters, and they don't count, 'cause Daddy—"

I cut my words short 'cause them other girls coming in the house. And I hope Mama don't mention nothing about me and Brother's surprise until after they leave. So Maybaby can't be in on it. But Mama go ahead and bring it up anyway.

"Annie Rye, Brother, I promised y'all a surprise. Now it's time y'all found out what it is. Me and your daddy decided that Doris, Brat, and Maybaby will be staying wit us from now on. So's we all can be a family."

I shift myself around and act like I'm straightening out the scarf on the mantelpiece. "You mean for always?"

"Forever," Mama says.

My throat feel all knotted up. And I squeeze water back behind my eyes. Some surprise. Doomsday. That's what it is. Doomsday. And nobody asked me nothing about nothing. I just don't count around here no more.

"Don't be standing there like a knot on a log. Come on over here and say something to your sisters, Annie Rye."

Since Mama told me I have to, I guess I better do it. But I'm sho not about to go all the way over where they is. I walk real slow halfway across the floor.

"Hey, Doris. Hey, Brat. Hey, Maybaby."

"Yeah." Brother pushes past me, grinning all over hisself. "Hey, y'all."

Soon as we all done with our Heys and everything, Mama tells them other girls, "Don't y'all go acting like no strangers. This your home too. Now go on in Annie Rye's room and put your belongings up. Y'all gon' be sleeping in there. Brother can sleep out here in the front room."

THEM 'pose-to-be sisters ain't done nothing but git on my nerves ever since they been here. Brat keep on hopping behind me, wanting to know how old I am. So I just tells her straight out, "Old enough to sleep in a bed without falling out." Shucks. Any dumb cluck could figure that out. We's all two years apart. Except for Brother and Elouise. So that means Maybaby was born after Doris. And Brat was born after Maybaby. And I come after Brat. Her and Brother just alike. Always asking eleven dozen questions. I can't even hear myself think around here. More than that, I can't even sleep in my own bed like I want to. Doris keep hogging up all the room. And just 'cause she the oldest, Mama says I have to mind her. That about make me puke up. Well, I'm gon' pay her no mind. And that goes double for Maybaby. She calling me now. Must be she don't know nobody else's name but mine. I pull the covers over my head and make like I don't even hear.

"Annie Rye, Mit say git up. All us up 'cept for you."

I lay still and makes out like I'm asleep. Anyhow, where she git on calling her Mit? All the rest of us calls her Mama.

"Annie Rye, stop playing possum."

I fling the covers off me. "How you know if I is or if I ain't? You ain't no mind reader."

Maybaby switches on out the room with her nose tooted up.

By the time I put my clothes on and everything, they all at the table. Brother is too. Setting over there grinning at Brat. That's her nickname. Her real one is Laura. "Laura Jean, the string bean, skinniest thing I ever seen." Look at her just licking that salt. That's why she look the way she do. She already skinnier than me. Pretty soon her blood gon' all dry up from licking that salt. Then she'll be setting around all wilted up.

"Here you a seat, Annie Rye." Brat points at a place next to her.

I don't care how much Mama call me "nice-nasty," I sho ain't setting beside Brat. She can offer all she want. I look around the table. "Somebody got my chair."

"Find yourself another seat, Annie Rye. It don't make no difference, long as you setting down." Mama talk across her shoulder and then go back to flipping flapjacks.

"You can set 'side me if you wanna." Brat tells me again, like I never heard her the first time. Shoot. I ain't had no choice. So I go ahead and set down.

"Mama done fixed some bacon to go 'long wit them flapjacks. It sho smell good, don't it?" Brat start inching around in her chair. "Bacon taste better than anything in the whole world."

"Not better than them jawbone breakers." Brother unloosen his bottom lip.

"Ah, anything's good to you. Long as you eating on it," I'm saying to Brother, when Brat go to hunching me with her elbow.

"Whatcha got for Christmas, Annie Rye?"

"My two front teeth," I tells her. She talk more than Brother do. Between the two of them, my ears not having no rest at all. I look off the other way, and Maybaby rolling her eyes dead at me. So I roll mine right back. Mama catch us giving dirty looks, and she don't waste no time setting us straight.

"Now listen here. I done had enough of this mess." Mama got her hands propped on her hips and tapping her foot on the floor. "Y'all ain't been together for more than a week and ya can't pass a decent word between you, unless one or the other snapping her head off. You act more like cats and dogs 'steada sisters, and it gon' stop. You hear me?"

"You sho right, Mama. Kinfolk ain't s'pose to be acting like they doing." Doris adds in her two cents worth.

Mama's foot still tapping on the floor. So I don't dare say what's in my mind. Chicken guts.

They just taking over everything. Even my place at the table.

After breakfast, Mama pull me aside. "You gon'

hafta try and git along with them, Annie Rye. Brat and them gonna be with us for a long time. Might as well git used to 'em and put your mind where it s'pose to be at. On your work."

That's why me and Brother out here so early in the morning. We got to slop Miz Soota. But she ain't even in the pen. Me and Brother take off across the field. We knowed right good where she'd be at. And sho nuff. Miz Soota in Mama's watermelon patch.

"Let's sneak up on her, Annie Rye, while she got her head down." Brother go tipping up on her. I do too. The next thing I know, we tangle up in vines and Miz Soota done took off the other way.

Mama must've heard all the commotion, 'cause she come running, waving her apron, just hollering. Miz Soota turns and head for the pigpen. Even Miz Soota know to straighten up and fly right when Mama hollers like that. Soon as she back where she s'pose to be, I plug up the fence.

"Listen here, Miz Soota," I says down low. "You best quit your busting out so much. Else you gon' be in a world of trouble." But I know she is already. I could tell 'cause Mama over there shaking her head. And I knowed Miz Soota done got on her nerves real bad.

"Will ya just look at my watermelon patch. If your daddy don't fix this fence I won't have nary watermelon fit to eat."

"That hog more trouble than she worth. Right, Mama?" Brother dust hisself off.

Mama ain't had no time to answer Brother back, 'cause Daddy done walked up. And I knowed he was gon' git a good blessing out.

"I'Lee, what in the world gonna become of my garden? Just look at it. Go ahead, look. My watermelons not half ripe yet—tore off the vines. Turnip greens all trampled over. Not to mention my black-eyed peas." Mama don't even stop to take a breath, she just go right on giving Daddy a piece of her mind. "I'Lee, I done told you more times than a little. Do something about that hog of yourn. Why don't you git rid of her?" Mama slings her arms in the air. "Mercy me, I can't see why you hang on to one hog when you got plenty more besides Miz Soota."

"Mit, you know Miz Soota just about the best hog we got for birthing pigs." Daddy bite off a chew of tobacco and goes on talking. "Come market time, her pigs always brings a fair price."

"I want you to know, Mr. Footman, this here garden help put food on the table too."

Now I knowed Mama was madder than a setting hen. She done gone and called Daddy "Mr. Footman."

"I know you done put in a lot of work in this here garden, Mit. I ain't disputing that. Baby, you know I appreciate it. But there's just no way I can afford to git rid of Miz Soota." Daddy push his hat back off his forehead. "I just hafta find a way to keep her penned up. That little money I got put away will come in handy right about now. Might as well git busy clearing way some of that back land, so's I can put up a new pen."

"Now, I'Lee, you know good and well that money s'pose to be for your baseball suit."

"I'll have more than enough left over to see about that too."

"Well, I reckon. If you say so."

"I say so. Now, how many times I done told you I'm the one s'pose do the worrying around here." Daddy puts his arms around Mama's shoulder. Me and Brother look at one another, 'cause we know everything gon' be hunka-dory.

"By the way, why you home this time of day?" Mama looks up at Daddy. "Don't tell me it's noon already. I ain't got one speck of food done. The hoecakes not even in the skillet yet."

"I come on back a bit early on account Miz Nettie want Annie Rye and Brother to clean out the turkey barn while I finish patching the shed. Says she'll give 'em twenty-five cents apiece. So I plan on taking them back wit me in the wagon, soon as I have me a little something to tide me over till suppertime."

"Well, they sho ain't going looking like they do. Go on in the house and wash up," Mama says to me and Brother. "Y'all look worse than Miz Soota do."

"And *we* more trouble than we worth too. Right, Mama?" Brother says right quick.

Mama looks up at Daddy, and they laugh. Then me and Brother start acting just like Miz Soota. Moving around, wagging our heads and grinning and oinking, all betwixt Mama and Daddy. Me and him still giggling when Brat walks up.

"Why you got such a long face?" Mama asks.

Brat hang her head down. "Ain't nothing to do."

Mama looks over at me. And I just fixing to tell her what all Brat could do around the house. But before I can open my mouth, Mama saying, "Annie Rye, why don't you see if Brat wants to go with you and Brother."

I don't say nothing. I just look at the ground.

"Annie Rye."

"Yes'm." I turn toward Mama.

"You hear what I just said?" Mama raise her eyebrows up. So I knows what I s'pose to say.

"Brat, you wanna come?"

She wanted to come all right. But it's not fair. Her tagging along with us. Shoot. I didn't have no chance to go off without them nowhere.

But I knowed Mama was gon' say if Brat don't go, me and Brother can't neither. I ain't wanted to miss my twenty-five cents, so I don't mention nothing about it when we climb on the wagon. I just set on the back and let my feet hang out like I always do, and make like she not even here. So it can be like it used to, with me and Brother back on the back and Daddy up there doing the driving. Sometimes I be glad we in the wagon instead of Daddy's Studebaker. Course, he don't use that none much anyway. Except when we go to Grandma's or to church, or to see him play baseball or something like that. He got it all dressed up with yellow bobbing birds, dancing dolls, and fancy flaps. And he got a big silver eagle setting right on the hood. Mama says she don't know which the closest to Daddy's heart—Miz Soota, his Studebaker, or baseball. But I be knowing which is closest to his heart. Me and Brother and Elouise and Mama. That's who. And nobody else. I roll my eyes over at Brat. Then I look over my shoulder at *my* daddy making that horse gitty-up.

"Hey, Daddy, we almost there yet?"

"Naw, Stompee. We got a little piece to go yet."

Stompee. That's a special name my daddy made up for me. When I was just a teen-ouncy little thing, Mama says every time Daddy go to picking on his guitar, I'd start stomping my foot. So after then he went to saying my made-up name.

I know we not nearly about there yet. I just wanted to be saying something so's I can hear Daddy say something back. We pass Gifford's house—he the colored man that stays up the road from us—

and we pass the spot where me and Daddy pick them bullets at, them big ole grapes that grow long in here. They all green now. And I ain't about to go asking Daddy nothing about when they s'pose to be ripe. 'Cause I ain't gon' start Brother to running his mouth or let Brat find out about them. So I dig down in my overalls and pull out my threaded button.

"You wanna chance?"

Brat hold her hand out, and I pass the thread to Brother. "And when you done, you hand it right back."

"What about Brat?"

"What about her?"

"She ain't had no turn."

I look Brother dead in the face and tells him straight, "Well, that's her b-i-z."

And then he go try and be all smart. "If Brat don't take no turn, I ain't neither."

"Suits me just fine." I snatch my thread back. If Brother want to be like that, let him. Ain't hurting me none. I roll my eyes at Brat. It's not enough Mama and Daddy on her side. Now Brother taking up for her too. Well, see if I care.

I swing my legs inside the wagon and prop them with my arms around them. Then I shut my eyes and wish hard as I can them 'pose-to-be sisters wasn't even here. I mean I done my champeen wishing. I even bat my eyes three times, like Grandma done told me to do when that ole boogie man scares me outa my sleep. But when I open my eyes, Brat still setting in the wagon. So I try to think up something else so's she won't be tagging behind me all the time. And before I can git it halfway thought up, I hear Daddy telling the horse to "whoa."

Don't seem like we oughta be at Miz Nettie's yet, but I guess we is. 'Cause I see her standing in the doorway. She Mr. Myszell's wife. And most the land down here in these piney woods belong to them.

Miz Nettie go to beckoning for us to come up to the house. So me and Brother climb down. Brat do too. I don't know what for. Nobody ain't said nothing about her helping out. And I'm sho not splitting my money up.

Before we come up to the porch good, I can tell Miz Nettie got her hair done up in what white folks call pin curls, and her face look like she done wiped flour all over herself. But I don't ask if she do or not. Mama says it ain't good manners to go prying into other folks' business and talking what I don't know. So I just listen up good to what Miz Nettie want me and Brother to do.

When we all done cleaning up behind them turkeys and straightening up in the barn, Miz Nettie gives me twenty-five cents. She gives Brother the same thing. Then she turn around and hand Brat five cents. A whole nickel. And she never said nothing about Brat doing nothing in the barn. Not one word. All Miz Nettie said was, "So you Mit's other daughter," and patted Brat on the head. And now she gits a nickel. And all she been doing over there is making ugly faces at Brother and giggling and going on. But if Miz Nettie wanna give her money away for nothing—that's her b-i-z.

Miz Nettie say we can find Daddy over at the sugarcane mill with Mr. Myszell. And I spot him right off, standing amongst some men. Mostly they was all colored, with a few white ones mixed in. But I could tell which one was Mr. Myszell. 'Cause he the only man I ever knowed that walk around with his Sunday-go-to-meeting clothes on instead of his everyday ones.

I see Mr. Tom Gifford too. He standing over next to Daddy, with a match stem sticking outa his mouth like he always do. That's when I hear Mr. Myszell telling Daddy about this new man that done come to live on one of his places.

"Ira Lee, this here's Josh Lampkins. He'll be working with y'all here at the cane mill come harvest time."

"Howdy, Mr. Lampkins." Daddy put his hand out to shake, but the white man don't take it. He just let his arms rest on top of his belly, that's sticking out from under his shirt, and go on talking to Mr. Myszell.

"I just need ya to point out who'll be running things at the mill here. I ain't got time to be standing here jawing all day. I need to be gitting on with my business."

Mr. Myszell clears his throat. "Ira Lee, here, oversees the goings-on here. So he's the one that'll be showing you how things oughta be done."

Mr. Lampkins' eyebrows go up. "I ain't used to taking orders from no . . . I mean, where I come from they ain't in the habit of just letting anybody be in charge. And I ain't gonna be taking the blame for something that don't git did right."

Daddy don't say nary word. He just shuffle his foot around in the dirt and spit tobacco juice.

"Well, you won't have to worry none. Ira Lee's a good man." Mr. Myszell slap Daddy across the back. "And he know about making cane syrup and sugar like he know the back of his hand."

Mr. Lampkins must not have liked what Mr. Myszell done said, 'cause he look at Daddy real hard.

"Well, Lampkins, what's it gonna be?" says Mr. Myszell. "You wanna take me up on my offer or not?"

"Like I done told ya, since my wife passed and left me wit three younguns, I needs a place to settle so's I can raise 'em up good and proper. Yeah, I'll be staying. Seeing how I don't have much choice."

"Good. Then it's settled. You go ahead and git yourself situated. And I'll be checking with ya later on."

Brother go to jerking on me and twisting around

with his legs crossed up. I figures I best take him on to the outhouse so's he can use it. Mama don't like for him to hold his water too long, 'cause he might pee on hisself.

Daddy already got the wagon turned around when me and Brother come back. And Brat done climbed herself right up on the seat next to him. So I says, "Girl, you might as well climb yourself right on in the back. 'Cause that's where I'm riding at."

Brat hang her head down and crawl across the seat.

"Stompee, there ain't no cause for you to be carrying on like you doing. We got enough trouble with the likes of Mr. Lampkins. No sense making more for ourselves." Daddy give me a hard look.

When we make it back to the house, Mama and them setting around in the front room. Time I walk in, Maybaby saying, "Go ahead, ask her. She know she done it."

"Done what?" I want to know, frowning up my face. "What y'all talking about?"

"Your daddy's meat," Mama says. "I was saving it for his supper tonight. It's all gone. Ain't nothing left but the meat skin."

"She know. She just trying to be sly wit it," Maybaby says.

"Maybaby, I'll handle this," Mama tells her. "Now, I aim to find out who been sneaking around in the kitchen."

"It was Annie Rye, just like I told you," May-baby says right off.

"Don't be so quick to lay the blame on some-body." Mama straightens her out.

"Well, earlier today she was the last one to come out the kitchen at dinnertime." Maybaby pops off at the mouth again.

I roll my eyes. "That don't mean nothing."

"It do if you had grease all around ya mouth."

"Maybaby, you always watching somebody," I hollers out. "Why don't you take care of your own-self?"

"Annie Rye, there's no need for raising your voice. Simmer down." Mama's eyebrows git all scrunched up.

I take me a deep breath and lean back on the set-tee next to Doris. And she looks right pass me at Mama. "I hate to say this, but I seen Annie Rye coming out the kitchen chewing on something just before they left for Miz Nettie's."

"But I didn't touch Daddy's meat."

"No sense trying to wiggle out of it," Maybaby decides. "We all know what you been up to."

Brother lean right up next to me. "Yep, Annie Rye, I seen you too."

"Boy, git outa my face."

"Young man, go somewhere and set yourself down, before you be in a world of trouble." Mama lets him know he's not off the hook yet neither.

And all the while I'm trying to tell her that piece of meat was left on my plate when we ate this noon, "Miz Flip" saying, "Yeah, sho it was."

"Mama, make Maybaby shut up. She just trying to pin the blame on me."

"I'm not trying to put nothing on you, girl."

"Yeah, you is too."

"Listen here." Mama slaps her hand across her lap. "This done gone far enough. I won't be raising my voice and hollering and going on. Some of y'all done ate up that meat. And if there's anything that bothers my mind more than a liar, it's somebody that's roguish."

Mama set back and cross one leg on top of the other. "And we can stay here all night long. Don't matter to me. Long as I come up with the truth."

"I didn't do it."

"Me neither," Maybaby and Brother says one after the other.

Brat looks around at Doris and hunch her shoulders up. Then Doris cut her eyes at me. "It seems to me," she starts off, "and I don't mean to lay blame on her, but Annie Rye was going in and out the kitchen all while everybody else was done. Even after her and Brat had cleaned the kitchen up. And she been eating on meat way after all us finished at the table. And it don't seem fair all us being punished 'cause she won't tell the truth."

Mama look at me one-sided, so I knows to speak

up fast. "But I am telling the truth. Sho I was going in the kitchen a lot. That's 'cause my throat was dry. I was dipping me some water out the bucket before we had to leave on the wagon."

"Girl, you oughta quit telling your stories." Maybaby lean back and cock her head. "Guess that means you won't be going possum hunting, don't it?"

"Maybaby, one more word outa you, and you'll be standing in the corner till this time tomorrow. I can handle this. Thank you, ma'am. Annie Rye . . ." Mama question me with her eyes. "What you hafta say for yourself?"

"Nothing. Ain't no use trying to prove nothing, 'cause you ain't believing me nohow." I hang my head down and look at the floor.

"All right, Miz Lady. March yourself on out to the smokehouse. Brother, bring me my switch."

I trail Mama out towards the back door, water rising up in my eyes, when Brat come up behind us.

"Annie Rye ain't done nothing. I the one ate up the meat."

chapter 5

Possum Hunting

>>>>>>>>>>>>>>>>>>>>>>>>>>>>>>>>>

I STILL can't figure it out. Brat done stuck up for me. She sho nuff did. That's why me and Brother git to be out here possum hunting with our granddaddy. Just me and him. And nobody else. Just like it used to be.

"Granddaddy . . . ?" Brother says, like he got something on his mind he can't figure out. "Granddaddy, why we going possum hunting at night? If we go in the daytime, we could see 'em better."

" 'Cause this when they be out prowling about, Jitterbug."

"Then what they do in the daytime? Maybe they be taking a nap. Right, Granddaddy?"

"I reckon they be resting up. Can't rightly say. But more than likely them rascals thinking up some sly tricks. They be right still, and if you ain't got no possum-hunting know-how, they fool ya just like that."

Brother run ahead with ole Duke and Trixy. "I smart too," he hollers back. "Just like them ole possums."

The moon done come out now, and long black lines stretch out across the ground. And a ways off in the woods, I hear them hounds just howling.

Granddaddy whistles, and they come back where we at. Brother do too. And I want to know why Duke and Trixy not siccing us a possum. Granddaddy says I don't have nothing to worry about, 'cause he knowed just where they'd be at. Right over yonder in them bushes, trying to find some blackberries.

So while ole Duke and Trixy smelling them out, all us set down next to Granddaddy's fire, on some croaker sacks he done brung along to tote that possum home in. Granddaddy brung sweet 'tatoes too. And soon as he lay them on the fire, he go to talking.

"It went like this," Granddaddy say, and I git my ears all tuned up 'cause I knows me and Brother fixing to hear something about them olden days.

"Back when yo' pappy was no bigger than a hog's swallow," Granddaddy goes on, "Randle Footman—my pappy—was half-cropping wit Kada Copsey. That's what they used to call sharecropping back then—half-cropping. Ole Kada had hisself a fine red horse wit a white splotch setting right between his eyes. Now, ole Kada knowed how much my pappy admired that horse. So one day he comes up to the house and says, 'Randle, I needs them snap beans picked by Saturday morning.' Now, this was already Friday evening, and he figured, even wit all us pitching in, there was no way under the sun Pappy was liable to finish up on time. So ole man Copsey makes him a bargain. 'If ya can have 'em ready, I tell ya what I'm going to do. I'm gonna letcha have Red, here.' For a while Pappy ain't saying nothing. He just stands there wit his hands in his pockets. Then he says, 'Mr. Copsey, I gotta think on this some. You knows I ain't spry as I used to be.'

" 'Aw, you can still kick up ya heels wit the best of 'em'—ole Kada keeps on talking—'and to show you my good intentions, I'm gonna throw in my buggy to boot. But if you ain't done when I comes for 'em, you lose yo' share.' Now, everybody knowed, all over the Negro quarters, ole man Copsey was a man of his word. So Pappy and ole Kada shook on it.

"Well, it seems Saturday rolled around quicker than a owl's eye. And 'fore Pappy knowed it, Mr. Copsey come riding up on Red, bright and early. And Pappy's setting on the front porch, whittling.

" 'Figured on finding ya in the field,' ole Kada says right off.

" 'No need,' Pappy says.

" 'And you knows you won't be having yo' share?' Mr. Copsey slides down off Red.

"Pappy don't say a mumbling word. He just walks on out back. Still whittling.

" 'One thing I likes about you, Randle, boy. You knows when ya licked.' Now ole man Copsey grinning ear to ear. And Pappy steady whittling. When they git around back, ole man Copsey cut his grin short. Them patches was picked clean and them snap beans all loaded on the wagons.

" 'How you done it?' Ole man Copsey go to scratching his head. And Pappy tells him how he made a big fire at the edge of the patches and dipped cattails in some grease and tied 'em on some poles and stuck 'em alongside each row, then set 'em on fire. Pappy go to telling him how them patches light up clear as day and how all us pitched in and worked all night long. Ole man Copsey looks Pappy square in the face, and Pappy don't flinch nary eyebrow. Then ole man Copsey starts to chuckle real soft like. 'Randle, you a sly ole rascal.' And he slaps Pappy across the back. 'They's yourn. The horse. And the buggy.'

"Yes sirree. You had to be up pretty early in the morning to outsmart Pappy. 'Cause he could out-slick the britches off the best of 'em." Granddaddy split the last sweet 'tato between me and Brother. Before I can put it in my mouth, ole Duke and Trixy start barking. So all us light out for the blackberry bushes, 'cause we know them hounds done spotted something for sure.

And soon as Granddaddy hold up the lamp, sho nuff—there's that ole possum, hanging upside down. Since Grandma don't be liking it when they shot full of holes, I climb right upside where he got his tail curled around a limb, so's I can shake him loose. I shake that tree a good fashion. And before I knows it, that ole possum hit the ground and take off.

"Sic him, Duke. Don't let him git away." I call out.

I drop down out the tree and haul tail where Granddaddy's lamp shining at, and that ole possum's cornered good. Now all Duke have to do is crawl in that hollow log and drag him out. And that possum's ours sho as gravy.

chapter 6

Sticks and Stones

>>>>>>>>>>>>>>>>>>>>>>>>>>>>>>>>

NEXT MORNING before my feet hit the floor good, Grandma got that possum smelling all over the house, and my mouth just watering. Then for no reason, Brother start bragging on them half-sisters, and mess my appetite up just listen at him.

"Yeah. And Brat took up for Annie Rye so's she wouldn't hafta git no whipping."

I wheels around face-to-face with Brother. "I ain't asked her to." I wall my eyes up at the loft. "Anyways, I don't need her to go sticking up for me. I can take up for myself."

Grandma steady spooning up pot liquor and dumping it back on the possum. "Nobody lives in this world all by theyself. We all need somebody some way, shape, form, or fashion. And there's no gitting around it."

"But, Grandma, we was doing just fine before they come barging in. This our family—mine's, Brother's, and Elouise's. And they just messing up everything. I wish they'd go back where they come from, so's things can be like they used to."

Now Grandma lay her spoon down and comes over to where I'm at. "Annie Rye," she says to me, squatting down on the floor, "you done seen how a hen spread her wings, so's her biddies can git under 'em. And no matter how many biddies there is, that hen's wings stretches so every one of them biddies fit, so's there's room for just one more. That's how it is wit a family. Its arms can spread to hold just one more." Grandma takes me by my shoulders. "You know what I'm talking 'bout?"

"I think so, Grandma." Water start running down my face, and Grandma dry it with the corner of her apron.

"Grandma . . . ," I says as she fixing to stand up. "Grandma . . . I love you a heap."

"Me too." Brother come over where we at. "I loves you a heap too, Grandma."

Grandma gives me and him a good squeezing, just as tight as can be.

EVER SINCE then I had it in my mind to act like Grandma done told me. But I ain't been back home no time before Maybaby go to meddling with me.

"Annie Rye, you oughta be shame of yourself, plaiting Elouise's hair like that. All sticking up like two cow horns. Look worse than yours do."

"Why don't you look at your ownself," I yell at her. "You don't look good. You don't look bad. You look like something the buzzards done had."

The next thing I know, Daddy's standing in the door. "What's the matter in here?"

"Nothing, I'Lee," Maybaby says right quick. "I was just showing Annie Rye how to underbraid Elouise's hair."

"Say, that looks real nice," Daddy says, peeping over Maybaby's shoulder at Elouise's head. "Stompee, you watch so's she can learn you how to fix it like she do."

"Yes sir, Daddy." I bite on my lip, so's I won't say nothing back. 'Cause I'm gonna be in hot water if I do. And by the look on Daddy's face, I know he got something else on his mind. So I act like I don't know nothing about nothing. Then Daddy looks dead at me.

"Any y'all seen my chewing tobacco? Can't seem to put my hands on it." Daddy go to patting on his overalls.

"No sir, Daddy. I ain't laid eyes on it since I give it to you the last time."

Maybaby jump up and run over to the mantelpiece. "Here it is, I'Lee. I done cut you some already."

"You gitting right handy to have around." Daddy

69

gives Maybaby a pat on the back, and she go to grinning all over herself. Who she think she is anyway? And where she git on cutting off Daddy's tobacco? I s'pose to do that. Now I'm so mad I could spit. Ahhh, chicken guts! And that goes double for Maybaby.

Shoot. Before I know it, Daddy'll be learning her to chunk better than me. Pretty soon I'm not gonna have noplace at all. Like the other day. She almost broke her neck racing to bring Daddy a drink of water. And she knows good and well I'm the one s'pose to wait on my daddy. And nobody else. I know what Maybaby's up to. I sho nuff got her pegged right. Trying to git on Daddy's good side.

But I can't figure Brat out. All this time we been back from Grandma's house and she didn't even said nothing about why she stuck up for me. And how come she saved me from that whipping. 'Specially when she could've got off scot-free. All she been talking about is going to the mailbox to see if that catalog ordering book done come. And now she can't go 'cause she and Maybaby have to help out with the crops. Mama said since they only need two more field hands, me and Doris could go next time around. So Brat wants to know if I'd save her some pictures, so's she can cut her out some paper dolls too. So I tells her I'll think about it. Then she wants me to say I promise. So I says I promise.

Later on, me and Doris head to the mailbox. Brother come too, hauling Elouise in his wagon.

I'm grinning and skipping out in front so's I can hurry up, 'cause I want to see if the mailman done brung us another ordering book. I go to strutting around like I got high-heel shoes on. Acting like I one of them fancy ladies in them ordering books. Just switching between the mailboxes and going on.

"Hey you! Whatcha doing fooling wit our mailbox?" A white boy poke his head out from behind a tree. And I nearly about jumps clean out my skin. Then I see it's J.D., that Lampkins boy. And I know he's up to no good. Seems like every single time we have to git our mail, they show up. Them Lampkins chillun ain't been nothing but trouble since they come meddling and going on.

"Seems like the cat done got her tongue." Now that bony J.D. got hisself right in my face.

"Negroes don't know B from a bullfrog. So what on earth they coming to the mailbox for?" That Ginny come across the cow pasture, with that little Sissy girl running behind her. Ginny the biggest one. Just like Doris. But it don't seem like it. The way she act.

"No sir. Can't read a lick," she say, running off at the mouth.

So I holler out, "I can too read. My mama send me to Mount Calvary School."

"And whatcha learning, little darkie? How to wait on us white folks?"

"They ain't gotta learn that, J.D. They know that's all they *fitting* for. It's just like Pa always done told us. You gotta kick 'em around a little so's they stay in they place. Otherwise they start having notions they better than us decent folks."

J.D. go to sniggling. But it don't tickle me none. Not one bit. So I roll my eyes at him real hard.

Doris can tell I'm boiling mad, so she says, "Just pick up the mail and come on, Annie Rye. Don't pay 'em no attention."

Soon as I pull the lid down, Ginny pushes past. "White folks first." So I just go ahead and let her be first. Then I reach in for ours and start back where Doris at.

"Not so fast." J.D. jumps right in front of me. "We ain't done witcha yet. We wanna know where y'all stole that wagon from."

"I ain't stole this wagon nothing. Daddy told Santa Claus to bring it for me." Brother speak up before I can say something back.

"Listen at the little darkie wit the pot gut." J.D. pokes Ginny with his elbow. "Everybody know there's no self-respecting Santa Claus gonna be caught dead in no darkie's house."

"You don't know nothing. Y'all just mad 'cause she don't have one." I cut my eyes at that little ole Sissy digging in her nose. "Y'all just too poor."

"Yeah." Brother jumps in. "Lookit them patched-up britches J.D. got on."

Ginny roll her eyes at us real hard. "We may be poor. But least we ain't no nigger."

"And ain't no nigger got no business having nothing better than us white folks," J.D. adds up. "So move that gal out that wagon. So's we can give Sissy a ride." J.D. waves for that little Sissy girl.

"You ain't touching my wagon. No sirree. You sho ain't." Brother back his wagon up, and Doris take the handle.

"Ahhh, let these darkies go on home. They ain't worth nothing anyways." J.D. steps to the other side, and that's when Maybaby and Brat come running up to where we at.

"Look here, boy. We sick and tired of y'all messing wit us." Maybaby got her finger wagging right in J.D.'s face. "And we not gon' be taking no more stuff off y'all neither."

J.D. standing there with his hands in his pockets. Acting like he a big shot. "Y'all knows better than to go round sassying us white folks. You best put a bridle on that tongue of yourn."

"Child, you must be outa your mind. 'Cause you got no business telling Maybaby how to use her tongue. She say what she please." Brat jumps up next to Maybaby, shaking her fist at J.D.

"Brat, Maybaby. Hush your mouth. Come on

here." Doris keeps calling 'em. But they keep right on standing in front of J.D. And J.D. keeps right on running off at the mouth.

"Look at these little darkies, will ya? They sho nuff got a little spunk to 'em. They mammy must've fed 'em some hot peppers for breakfast."

Ginny started laughing.

"Don't you go calling my mama no mammy." Maybaby got her fist all drawed back. She fixing to whop J.D. good. So Doris catch hold of her arm and pulls her off.

"Girl, you best cool yourself down, and let's go on home. Brat take Brother's wagon so's we can hurry up."

All us doing like Doris done said, when I hear J.D. say, "Hey, nigger! This for you!" And a rock nearly about hit Brother's wagon.

"Better keep this rock to make you some soup." I chunks it right back.

"Annie Rye. You quit that."

"But they throwed at her first," Brat tells Doris.

"And he better be glad I ain't used the dip-see-do Daddy done showed me. Else he'd be having a hickey knot right upside his head."

"Makes no never mind who throwed first." Doris put Elouise on her hip. "And you best mind me, Annie Rye. And Maybaby, I thought y'all s'pose to be working."

"They let us off early. So me and Brat come to meet y'all."

"Come to start something, you mean."

"We didn't start nothing, Doris, and you know it. Every time we come to the mailbox, they always bothering us. And we never done nothing to 'em." Maybaby try to make Doris see how it is. But Doris keep talking the same talk.

"We s'pose to keep outa trouble and not start nothing. Sometimes it's best just to let things be and not add wood to the fire."

"I don't know nothing about all that." I push my lip out, pouting. "All I know, if you big enough to pass a lick, you big enough to take one back. And I ain't no nigger." I kick hard at the ground. "And if they call me that another time"—my eyes fill with tears—"I gonna—"

"You gonna hush up and quit slowpoking around. So's we can git on home." Doris look at me all mean like. She don't have no business being mad at me. But I hush up like she done told me. 'Cause I mad too. Madder than a setting hen.

Come suppertime, I still thinking about it. So I mention to Daddy about them white chillun picking at us. Chunking rocks and all. And he says he ain't gonna have us picking no fights. Else he'll be giving us something so we won't be setting down for a month of Sundays.

So I tells him real fast, "Naw sir, we ain't been starting no fights."

Then Brother opens his mouth. " 'Cept for Annie Rye picked up—" I kick at him underneath the table, so he'll hush.

"And where was you when all this was going on, Doris? You s'pose to keep your eyes on these younguns and make sho they don't be in no devilment."

"I brung 'em right on home, Mama."

"She sho nuff did, Mit. And if you ask me, them white chillun deserve just what they got."

Mama cuts her eyes at Maybaby. "Didn't nobody ask you. And until somebody do, speak when you spoke to. Now, from now on y'all go to the mailbox later on in the day."

"But, Mama, it's too hot then." My face git all parched up.

"Never mind how hot it is. You heard what I done said."

"But, Mama, how come we hafta go when it be scorching hot out there? We didn't do nothing. Them white chillun started it."

"It ain't fair, Mit. It just ain't fair."

"One more word, Maybaby, and you'll find yourself standing in the corner with no supper." Mama look at me one-sided, and I knowed not to pitch a fit. Wouldn't do no good nohow.

So I just says, "I ain't hungry. Can I be scused from the table?"

Mama look at Daddy, and he tells me to "go on."

On the way in the other room, I hear Mama say, "Lord knows, we don't need no trouble with these white folks."

chapter 7

Trouble in the
Piney Woods

>>>>>>>>>>>>>>>>>>>>>>>>>>>>>>>>>>>>

FROM THEN ON, we go for the mail like Mama
done told us, when the sun so hot it about fries our
brains. That's why I sho was glad when ole man
Myszell told Daddy he could use me and Doris in
his tobacco barn for a spell. I was glad, too, 'cause
I reckon we rid of them Lampkins. But I guess I
must've reckoned wrong. 'Cause Ginny there too.
Me and Doris is just minding our own business when
she haul off and says, "Whatcha doing bringing them
nigger babies in this here barn? Git 'em on back
home." Ginny point at Brother and Elouise, setting
behind us on a pallet.

Mama done give us a good talking to before we
left the house this morning, so me and Doris keep
on stringing tobacco. Acting like we never even heard

a word she was saying. Then she stand right in Doris face. "Did you hear me, pickaninny?"

"Go on, Ginny. Nobody's bothering you." Doris keeps on threading tobacco.

"You hard of hearing or something? I'm not gonna keep repeating myself, gal." Ginny shoves Doris. "Now take them nigger babies on out this barn."

"I'll make *you* look like a nigger." Doris wheels around. And before I knowed it, she all over that girl like white on rice.

A whole bunch of people crowd around, and a white man start shoving them back. Big Jake. He snatch on Doris and sling her across the barn. Doris hit the wall and slide down in the dirt.

"You come to this here barn to work. Not stir up trouble." Big Jake standing right over Doris. "But since you can't figure out which is which, don't let me catch none a y'all around here no more. Not long as I'm overseeing this here tobacco barn. Now git."

Big Jake help Ginny off the ground. "You OK, Miz Ginny?"

"Who she think she is, jumping on me like that?" Ginny go to dusting herself off.

"Don't ya worry none," Big Jake tells her. "I done taught 'em a lesson."

ALL THE WAY HOME, I keeps thinking we in real hot water this time. And I just know we gon' git it good. Boy, just you wait until Mama hear tell about this.

And it sho didn't take long neither. 'Cause Mama meet us on the front porch when we make it to the house.

"Doris, you done gone and lost every sense in your head? Huh, gal? What on earth possessed you to beat up on that white girl like that?" Mama hold the door open so we can go in the house.

"Tom Gifford got the word and drove over. News like this don't take long to spread. And here I am thinking I might have a little peace and quiet." Mama just fussing. "Now this. Lord have mercy. What next? And Doris you know better. What done come over you?"

Doris don't say nothing. She don't even try to take up for herself. She just keep on picking at her hands.

So I speaks up. "It was all that Ginny's fault, Mama. She started the whole thing. We wasn't doing nothing. Nothing a 'tall. And Ginny just come flouncing herself up in Doris face, and Doris set her down. That's all."

"Gal, when I want your pot to boil, I'll let you know. Now git somewhere and set yourself down." Mama wags her finger at me and go back talking to Doris. "I'm listening."

"Well, we was doing our work, when Ginny go calling us names."

"And she called Elouise and Brother nigger babies," I put in.

Mama give me a hard look. "Doris talking, Annie Rye. And I won't tell you another time to quit butting in."

"Yes ma'am." I knowed not to keep on dipping in, 'cause Mama done told me to hush more than once already. And I don't say another word—not nary one—so's Doris can finish telling Mama what been going on.

"So then she shoves on me, and I—"

"And Doris beat that girl up and give her a black eye. Just like Joe Louis." Brother go to bouncing around the floor with his fist balled up.

Mama must've got a bad headache from somewhere, 'cause she set down, holding her head. And boy, did she give us a blessing out.

"Y'all better walk a chalk line, else I'm gon' put something on you Grandma's washing powder ain't gonna take off."

Later on, when Maybaby come in out the field, she start saying that white girl got just what she deserve. Maybaby would've got a whipping, except Daddy took up for her. Now, Brat and me and Brother setting out on the front porch with our hands propped up to our jaws, trying to stay outa trouble, when ole man Myszell and Mr. Lampkins rolls up.

"Your pa here?" Mr. Myszell says right off.

"Yeah, he here," Brother tell him.

"Then make haste. Go fetch him, boy," Mr. Lampkins snaps at Brother.

So he take off around the house and come back holding on to Daddy's britches. "See, Daddy. I told you some white men was here."

"Howdy, Mr. Myszell. Mr. Lampkins." Mr. Lampkins don't even open his mouth to speak. So Daddy don't waste no more words on him.

"What can I do for you, Mr. Myszell?"

"You can learn them younguns of yourn some manners," Mr. Lampkins breaks in.

"Ira Lee, I understand there was some confusion in the barn this morning," Mr. Myszell says.

"Yes sir. It seems Mr. Lampkins here—his girl was pushing my chillun around and they took up for themselves."

"That's not the way I heard it," Mr. Lampkins says right quick.

"Well, maybe you heard wrong," Daddy tells him.

"My Ginny Sue setting over yonder all black and blue, can hardly see out one eye, and you mean to tell me them younguns of yourn not at fault?"

"I tell my chillun never start no trouble. I tell 'em too, never run from none neither."

Mr. Lampkins give Daddy a mean look. "Boy, you done bit off more than you can chew."

Daddy roll his tobacco around in his mouth and spit juice beside Mr. Lampkins' boot.

Mr. Lampkins' face turn red as fire. "You gitting too big for your britches, sonny boy."

"In that case, why don'tcha give me a little slack?"

Mr. Lampkins step toward Daddy. And Daddy don't flinch nary eyelash. Not nary one. He just looks him dead in the eye.

"Myszell, you best do something about this uppity nigger of yourn."

"Look here, Lampkins, there'll be none a that kind of talk long as you working for me. Understand? And till I git to the bottom of this, your younguns nor Ira Lee's can work in the barn."

Mr. Lampkins' lip go to twitching like a mule. Then he drags off, mumbling to hisself. But we all hear what he saying. "More than one way to skin a cat." Then he look back. "Or a nigger."

So Mr. Myszell hollers at him, "I'm warning you, Lampkins. If there's any trouble, you move out."

But I knowed there'd be more trouble. Big trouble. I could just feel it in my bones. And I knowed Daddy figured on it too. 'Cause by the time ole man Myszell leave our house, Daddy setting in the back door all by hisself, picking on his guitar.

Nobody feel much like eating no supper or nothing. Except for Brother. So all us set around on the back steps, looking at the sun finish going down and listening at Daddy playing on his guitar and singing the blues.

And I sho wanna stay up too. So I try to tell Mama I'm not nodding off. My head just won't be still like it s'pose to, 'cause my neck weak from bending over these steps. But she makes me go on to bed anyhow.

By the time I put my sleeping clothes on, I'm all woke up for real. Now I remembers. About them white folks calling us nigger. Daddy says there ain't nothing wrong with being colored. It's what you got on the inside that makes you what you is.

Anyway, Mama always say somebody else running this show. And then she tells me about cousin Effie, the one that lives way up north, and about them trees they got up there that turn all kinds of colors. She says them trees is the prettiest sight you ever laid eyes on. And God make them trees. And he made all us people, just like them trees. Some one color and some another. And she told me He loves all us the same. Just like we is.

But something still keep bothering my mind. Why He let them white folks treat us like they do? Mama just says when the time is ripe, God gon' lead His people out this oppression just like He led His other ones out the land of Egypt. Then her eyes turn all watery and she go to mourning and singing like Great-Grandma Moriah do. And I hear them slavery time songs in my head. I hears Grandma Moriah clear as day. Mourning and rocking. Mourning and rocking. My eyes go shut, and the mourning seems far away.

chapter 8

Cross Burning

>>

BEFORE I KNOW what's happening, I'm wide
awake. Setting straight up. The whole room bright
as day. Like somebody done light a whole bunch of
kerosene lamps. Then I figures it out.

"Fire! Ma-ma! The house on fire!" I almost trip
over myself, gitting in the living room.

"Hush your mouth, gal. And be still." Mama grab
hold to my sleeping clothes. Her and Doris just
standing around the floor, letting the house burn up.

"But the house is burning!"

"No it ain't. Now do like you told. Hush." Mama
done already got her words out, but her mouth still
standing wide open. And I see why. Daddy toting
his double-barrel shotgun.

"I'Lee, you can't go out there." Mama let me loose and catch hold to Daddy.

"Ain't nobody gonna scare me off. Nobody." Daddy snatches his arm back. But Mama still got ahold of him.

"Turn me loose, Mit."

"I'Lee, listen at me. Mr. Myszell . . . he'll come and stop all this. He's a good man. You know he is. I'Lee please . . ."

"Yeah . . . and sometimes a good man can be too late."

I slip past Mama and them and peep out the window. A cross setting right out in our yard. Just burning like crazy. Before I can see anything else, somebody grab me. And I nearly about jump outa my skin.

Maybaby got hold of my arm. "Bring yourself away from that window, girl. You lost all your senses?"

"I'Lee done lost all his. He know what happened over in the next county," I hear Mama say, while Maybaby drag me back where she and Brat standing at.

I knowed what happened over in the next county too. About how that colored man got strung up by his neck.

But Daddy still tells Mama, "Makes no never mind. They just can't keep on pushing your face in

the hog trough and spect you to come up grinning."

"I'Lee, *please* . . ." Mama beg him real hard.
But Daddy not listening to her none. He keep right
on raising the top latch. Then he act like he done
heard something.

Now I hear it too. Footsteps. Somebody walking
up on the porch. Then he start banging on the door.
Daddy ease the latch back down in the slot and
cocks his gun.

"Mit, git them younguns in the kitchen."

Mama go to pushing all us where the kitchen at.
Just then somebody outside hollers out real loud,
"Open up. You hear me in there. Open up."

My heart start jumping just like a bucking horse.
I know they gonna bust the door right down. Gonna
bust it down for sho.

Daddy got his gun pointing straight at the door,
and the banging keeps on.

"Open up. . . . Ira Lee, it's me, Myszell."

Now all us turn around and come back where
Daddy standing with Mr. Myszell.

"Y'all all right?"

Daddy takes a deep breath and tell him, "Yeah,
we OK. I'm sorry about that, Mr. Myszell. But I
couldn't make out if it was you or not."

"No need to go 'pologizing, Ira Lee. I figured
something like this might happen. So I had a little

talk with the sheriff, and he's down the road a ways. We didn't see nobody when we come. Must've scared them off. But I have a good notion who's behind all this." Mr. Myszell clears his throat and pat Daddy on the back. "I'm real glad y'all OK."

Before he leave, Mr. Myszell check around outside the house and tell us to git some rest. But nobody do. Daddy sho don't. He never shut his eyes one wink all night long. He just set by the front door with his shotgun laying on his lap, looking at the door and listening.

Early next morning when Mr. Myszell come back with the sheriff, he bring a basket.

"Nettie thought y'all could do with a little something, Mit." He lay his hat on the mantelpiece and hand Mama what he done brung. "Some gingerbread in there too. She know how the younguns got a craving for it."

Mama take the basket and motion for us to follow her in the kitchen, while Daddy and them talk. I try to put my ear up to the door so's I can hear, but Mama give me a hard look, and I gon' and help unpack the food Miz Nettie done sent.

FOR A DAY or so, Mama won't let us outa her sight. Couldn't even much go on the porch unless she saying "Where y'all going?" So the first time we been allowed anywhere past the front yard, it's only 'cause we kept on begging. Mama say we could if we go on and pick up the mail and come straight back to the house. So that's what we all do. Brat and Doris, and me and Maybaby. And Brother, he just hafta tag along too. So we let him coast down the hill in his wagon so's he won't be straggling behind. 'Cause we know Mama ain't in no mood for no kinda foolishness. Her patience done wore plumb thin.

Her nerves been on edge real bad too. Nobody can't barely make a sound unless she jumping to see what's the matter. Can't much blame her none for acting the way she is. I sorta half spect J.D. to poke his head from behind a tree somewhere any minute. But from now on we ain't gonna have to worry none about running into them Lampkins while we at the mailbox. 'Cause they won't be living hereabouts no more. They done moved somewhere clear across the county. But there been some talk he still got it in for Daddy. 'Cause he say it's on account of Daddy he done got put off Mr. Myszell's place. I don't see why he want to go blaming Daddy. He done owned up to what he done. Burning that cross in front of our house and all. He says he ain't no nigger-lover, and he feels proud he ain't gonna be working for one neither. The colored folk say Daddy had better watch out, 'cause Mr. Lampkins got a lot of meanness in him. But Daddy says we ain't got nothing to be worried about.

So I guess we ain't. 'Cause I be knowing if somebody was to harm one hair on our head, Daddy
would be all over 'em. All over 'em like fleas on a
hound.

chapter 9

If It Ain't One Thing, It's Another

>>>>>>>>>>>>>>>>>>>>>>>>>>>>>>>>>>>

SINCE ALL the cross burning happened, we ain't been doing nothing much. Everybody mostly been just laying around the house taking it easy. Mama and them don't even have to go to the fields or nothing. Mr. Myszell says Daddy ain't to worry about it none, 'cause his other field hands will help out for a while. He says it's best Daddy stick close to the house, in case something might happen like it done night before last.

I yank up a clump of grass and dunk the roots in a can of water. "I think you gonna make a fine grass doll," I says, tying a rag around the middle part. "And you gon' be name Miz Susie Q. Wit you hair all curled up right pretty like, you'll be just like one a them fancy ladies who knows just how to strut, sho nuff." I wind the long, stringy roots on a stick and wait for them to turn under. "Umm-huh. You gon' be right fine. Right fine indeed." I hold Miz Susie Q out in front of me real proud like, admiring how fine she is, then lay her down and yank up another clump of grass. One day I'm gonna buy me a real baby doll. Spanking brand-new. Right after I save my pennies all up.

But I still like them grass ones I done made all by myself. Brat do too. That's why I made her one just like mine. Soon as she all done cleaning out the fireplace, we gonna take our grass dolls and go fishing. Just me and her. Seems to me she ain't half bad for a half-sister. And she just about my own size. So when we cut out paper dolls from the ordering books, she don't chew them up like Elouise do. And Brother's not much better. Boys don't know scat about anything like dress-up and playing with tea sets. But Brat do. And yonder she come with the hoe now.

"You ready to go hook some a them mudfish?" I hollers out.

"I ready if you is." So me and her start going out back so's we can dig up some baits. Before we halfway around the house, I hear Mama.

"I'Lee, I wish you'd hurry up and finish with that other pen. I'm sick and tired of Miz Soota messing up my garden. Just look at this." Mama hold up a half-dead vine in Daddy's face.

Daddy don't say nothing. He just shifts his to-bacco to the other side of his jaw.

"If this keeps up," Mama goes on, "I won't have no garden a 'tall."

"I intended to buy some of that chicken wire off the rolling store when it come through last time. But with all that's been going on with Lampkins, it slipped my mind. I just have to keep patching up the old one best I can until I go in to town." Daddy slides his cap to the front of his head. "I done boarded up just about every inch of that fence. And that dang hog always figures another way out."

"And this time all the other hogs gone too," Mama tells him.

Daddy spit tobacco juice. "Y'all younguns go find them hogs. I hafta fix the fence."

Me and Brat take off through the weeds, and Mama spread her apron on the ground so's she can put Elouise down. I can tell Miz Soota done got on Mama's nerves real bad, 'cause she over there fuss-ing to herself. "If it ain't one thing it's another. And that hog is gonna be the death of me yet."

Miz Soota done went and did it now. Done give Mama too much worration. And my whole day all messed up too. I didn't even have a chance to go fishing. No telling where them hogs is by now. Betcha they scattered every which way.

But after a while, me and Brat have them all back in the pen—all except Miz Soota.

"Where on earth is that hog?" I take in a deep breath and blows it out hard. "Brat." She way across the field. So I hollers out again. "Brat. You see any sign of Miz Soota yet?"

"Naw, I didn't see her a 'tall. Maybe she down in the woods."

"Yeah. And more than likely she done got herself bogged down in that mud pond and can't git herself out."

I head off towards the woods, and I see Mama standing off yonder beside a pine tree. So I figure Miz Soota must not be stuck or nothing. Mama just got her cornered. And boy, I sho is glad. 'Cause I'm tired of running behind her all the time. "She got her nerve," I says out loud. "Keep busting out that pen anytime she feels like it. Huh. I got me something else to be doing besides traipsing after her all day." I keep on talking to myself all the way where Mama is. But she's not trying to drive Miz Soota back or nothing. She just standing there, doing nothing. And I wonders why she got that funny look on her face, the way she done when I fell off the porch in the bushes. Then I sees Miz Soota. Blood oozing every which way.

"Dad-dy, down here! Miz Soota!" My voice echo way off in the woods, and before it dies down, Daddy's where me and Mama at. Brat too. Daddy takes one look at Miz Soota and figures it all out.

"She done got herself caught on barb wire.

Stompee, y'all go bring the wheelbarrow." I steady got my eyes on Miz Soota. Ain't hardly heard a word Daddy done said.

"Don't stand there gazing in space, gal!" Daddy hollers at me. "Git."

Me and Brat go up the hill and back so fast it nearly about make my head swim. And when Daddy pushing Miz Soota back in the wheelbarrow, I feel that funny feeling in the bottom of my belly. Like butter churning. And I know she in bad shape. I can tell 'cause I see that worried look on Daddy's face. And all the while he tending to Miz Soota he don't say nothing much except how that burnt motor oil out the car cure dog mange, and how it oughta help heal Miz Soota. Then he git all quiet again.

EVERY DAY Daddy doctor on Miz Soota, and me and Brat and Brother pull up some more weeds for Miz Soota to lay on. Daddy say the main thing to watch out for is screwworms. 'Cause blowflies can give 'em to her. And we keeping them off real good too. But Mama says it don't make no kinda sense nursing that hog like she people. And if we want to set out here, that's up to us. Long as we not using her church fans.

Daddy been saying seem like she doing OK. Then when he comes out to the pen this evening, he just shake his head and mumbles, "It ain't looking too good." And I knows Miz Soota done took a turn for the worse. Blowflies done give her screwworms. So Daddy mix up a batch of pine tar and turpentine to wipe it on with little mops he done made out of rags. Miz Soota don't grunt or nothing. She just lay still while Daddy do his doctoring.

"Don't you worry none, Miz Soota," I says. "Daddy gonna fix you up real good. Everything gonna be all right. You'll see."

And sho nuff, Miz Soota, she up and about in less than a week, eating slop and everything just like she used to. But I done told her don't be trying to overdo it, stirring around too much. 'Cause she might wear herself out and start feeling poorly again. It ain't been the same not having her poking her nose into something. But knowing her, she'll be up and busting out that ole pigpen any day now. I bet she just waiting for a chance to be in Mama's watermelon patch.

And this slop will really make her sit up and root. There she is over there, laying down. "See what I tell you, Miz Soota? Done plain wore yourself out. Git up and eat this here slop. So's you'll feel better."

Miz Soota don't pay me no attention. She just wanna do what she want to. "Miz Soota," I says again, "come on and git this stuff I done brung you. Don't you hear me, hog? Stop playing possum." But she don't move at all. So I ease up to where she laying at.

"Miz Soota . . ." Miz Soota don't say nothing. She don't even grunt.

"Ma-ma! Ma-ma!" I takes off like a buck rabbit. Mama meets me halfway, Brother at her heels.

"Miz Soota . . . slop . . ." I try to catch my breath, but my words come out all mixed up.

"Talk straight, gal! What's the matter witcha?" Mama grab hold to my shoulders.

"Miz Soota . . . She ain't gitting up, Mama. She ain't gitting up!"

chapter 10

Egg Suckers

>>>>>>>>>>>>>>>>>>>>>>>>>>>>>>>>>

MIZ SOOTA buried underneath that ole pecan tree down the hill yonder. But she's not under there no more. She sho nuff ain't. I rolls over on my belly and spit between my teeth.

> *"Bring out the sugar*
> *And bring out the tea—*
> *Miz Soota, Miz Soota,*
> *The blackest hog I ever did see—*
> *Black as soot in the chimney."*

She sho nuff was. And smart too. So I'm not worried none much. 'Cause I knows she doing right fine just where she is. But Brother won't believe one word I say.

"Annie Rye, you sho Miz Soota done got in hog heaven?"

"Brother, how many times I gotta tell ya. I'm sho as I setting here on this ground."

"And she got her own pea patch, wit some watermelons throwed in?"

"Yep."

Brother flop down on his wagon and fold his arms across his lap. "And you sho she got all that good stuff up there where she at?"

"Don't go worrying none," I tells him. "I done heard Reverend Jackson preach lots of times. And I knows just what to say to git Miz Soota in. You remember that time I baptized that chicken? Didn't I git her good and wet? Just like Reverend Jackson did Miz Hattie Bell down at the river."

Brother's eyes go to shining like marbles. "Yeah. And that chicken went to wobbling round and jumping just like Miz Hattie Bell did."

"See. What I tell ya? More than likely Miz Soota having herself a good ole time by now."

Brother's grin spread ear to ear. He still grinning when we come up to the front steps, where Doris and them setting at fixing they hair. Just as I start to set next to Brat, Brother go to hopping like a toada frog, stuttering and going on.

"Talk straight so's we can understand you," Doris tells him.

Brother's words won't come out right. They git tangled up in his mouth.

"What on earth you talking about, boy?" Maybaby says, walling her eyes up at the sky.

I can't figure out if Brother clowning around or if he having a honest to goodness fit. 'Cause he sho is acting strange. Maybe he done caught the heebie-jeebies from somewhere. I know one thing. He better straighten hisself up pretty quick. Else we gonna have to shoot him. Just like Grandma done her mule that time.

"We don't know a word you saying. Talk slow." Now Doris got Brother by the shoulders.

"Gu-gu-ess what, y'all. Annie Rye done prayed Miz Soota to hog heaven."

They all fall out laughing. Brat too.

So I tell them straight out, "I don't see nothing so funny."

"I do." Maybaby pops off at the mouth. "Heaven's for people, girl. Not hogs."

So I says right quick, "You ever been there?"

Maybaby twist her mouth to one side, looking all stupid.

"Well, then"—I look her dead in the face—"how you know so much about it?"

"Why you getting so hot under the collar for? Miz Soota weren't nothing but a dumb old hog anyway."

I jumps up. "Listen here, honey child. You better quit making fun of Miz Soota, or else you gonna git the pee slapped right outa you."

Maybaby hop right up in my face. "Do it, then."

"If there'll be any slapping going on, I'll be the one doing it." Mama standing right in the doorway. "Now both of y'all set yourself down somewhere."

I ease back down on the bottom step and chunks a clump of dirt across the road.

"Girl, quit that chunking. Got that sand flying in my face." Maybaby got her mouth running again. "Anyways, you might hit somebody."

"Not unless I'm aiming at 'em," I says, winding my arm above my head and slinging it out. "You see, one day I'm gon' be a pitcher, just like Daddy will be doing for the Boweevils come week after next."

"And we's gonna have us a good ole time. Parched peanuts. Jelly cake. And a chew of tobacco. So's I can spit just like Daddy do when he pitching." Brother go to jumping around, flapping his arms like chicken wings.

Me and Brat hop up and mock Brother. Doing just like he doing. Maybaby do too. But not Doris. She just set there with a strange look on her face. Then out a clear blue sky she says, "I don't think we going."

"We ain't?" Brother quit flapping his arms. "Why ain't we?"

Doris just fixing to answer him back, and I cut

her off. "You just making up a story." Now all us set back down on the step. "You just trying to trick us, ain'tcha?"

But I know Doris not doing no such thing. I can tell by the look on her face.

"Daddy ain't got no money for his baseball suit. He done used it all on that new hog."

"That's a crying shame." Brat drop her head and make squiggly lines in the dirt. "Daddy really had his heart set on it too. I sho wish we could do something so's he won't have to miss out. Only— we ain't got one red cent to our name."

Doris look over at Brat. "You got anything in mind?"

Brat push her shoulders up and let them fall back down. "Search me, Doris."

"Me too." Brother hunch up his shoulders just like Brat.

"I got some money," I say right quick. "I got ninety-five cents hid in my cigar box."

"Ahh, girl, that don't amount to dooly squat," Maybaby butts in.

"More than you got," I says right back.

"If I had some, I wouldn't put it with yourn."

I roll my eyes at her. "Nobody ask you to."

"Will y'all quit acting like two dogs at the same bone?" Doris got a frown on her face. "Act civilized. Now, we ain't got but two weeks before Daddy's suit comes C.O.D., cash on delivery. And we got to have the money by the time the mailman drop it off."

I know Doris ain't playing. I could tell by her voice. So I tries hard as I can to think up something. But I can't make nothing come in my mind. Nobody else can't think up nothing neither. So all us out here looking like sick chickens. And time I come up with a thought, it slip my mind, 'cause Mama's hollering asking where Doris at.

"Here I is, Mama. Over here 'side the house. You want me for something?"

"I sho do. I need you and Annie Rye to run this here mess of turnip greens up to Miz Nettie's. I been promising her some for the longest." Mama standing in the door, holding a paper sack in her hand. "Make haste and come on back here. Supper'll be ready in a little bit. So y'all ain't got no time to be visiting wit them Gifford chillun. You hear me?"

"We heard, Mama." Doris speaks right up. And me and her don't waste no time going on up the road. All the way, Daddy's suit running across my mind. So I ask Doris if she done figured anything out yet.

And she just says, "Where there's a will, there's a way. And I sho nuff got a will. And the Lord know the way."

Doris done gone to talking and walking so fast I have to skip to keep up. And I sho am glad to make it to Miz Nettie's so I can rest a spell on the veranda. Those white folks don't call it no porch, 'cause it goes nearly about halfway around the house.

I see Miz Nettie got company, and I knows I ain't s'pose to be setting under no white folks' nose. 'Specially around Miz Bradshaw. Seeing how her husband is a big shot in these parts. So I go way down to the other end and take me a seat, while Doris goes where Miz Nettie and them setting at.

"Howdy do, Miz Nettie. Miz Bradshaw." Doris hold up the paper sack. "Mama done sent you this here package. She says she sorry it took her so long to git around to it."

"That's just fine, Doris. Why don't you put it inside the kitchen, so they keep cool."

Doris beckon for me. I git on up and go in the house so's she can put Miz Nettie's turnip greens up.

I can see Miz Bradshaw out the kitchen window. Looking like she done mashed up some red berries and rubbed them all over her jaws. But I ain't gonna mention nothing about it. 'Cause Mama done told me more times than a little about talking about what I don't know. Miz Nettie pour Miz Bradshaw a glass of lemonade and tells her how she in a pickle 'cause Maggie, her hired girl's mama, took sick. Now she don't have nobody to help out in the house for a while.

Me and Doris look at one another at the same

time. And I know we thinking the same thing. So me and her go back out the veranda where Miz Nettie and them setting at.

"Pardon me, Miz Nettie." Doris standing with her arms drawed behind her back. "If you be needing some help, me and my sisters willing to work for you until Maggie come back."

Miz Nettie studies Doris up and down. And I know she not gon' be making her mind up easy. That's why I standing over by this bannister with my fingers crossed.

After a while, Miz Nettie lean back and unscrunch her forehead. And I know she done made her mind up. And when she come right out and say she'd give us a try, Doris must've thanked her eleven dozen times before we headed on home.

And soon as me and Doris walk in the door, Brother start being nosy. "What y'all had? Gingerbread?"

"Who said we had something?" I gives him a question right back.

"I know y'all had something. I can tell 'cause y'all grinning. And I bet y'all had gingerbread too, 'cause every time me and Annie Rye go to Miz Nettie's she give us some."

"That don't mean we got none," Doris tries to tell Brother. But he's not listening at a word she saying. He drag a chair over where we at and stands on it.

"Lemme smell your breath, then."

"Boy, if you don't move yourself out my face, you better." Doris set him straight. "And if you don't quit acting the way you doing, you ain't gon' never know what we got."

Brother slide down in the seat and suck his lip.

Doris scooch in beside him. "Now let me tell you what we got."

Brother's eyes grow big as walnuts.

Then Doris tells him, all proud like. "We got us a job."

Brother turn around and look at her like she done lost all her sense. "You mean y'all ain't got no gingerbread a 'tall?"

"Nope. We gonna be working for Miz—"

Before Doris can finish her words out, Brat and them huddle where we at.

"You mean you gonna be paid some money?"

Brat act like she's not believing her ears. So Doris go on and tell them all about how Miz Nettie want all us at her house bright and early in the morning. And how we'll make five dollars a week for cleaning and ironing, and twenty-five cents apiece for them that do the turkey barn.

"For real, Doris? For true? You hear that, Maybaby? Hot dog!" Brat snap her fingers. "Daddy's suit good as got."

"Don't go being so glad," says Maybaby. " 'Cause y'all gonna be shoveling out that turkey barn. Me and Doris working in the house."

Now Maybaby done got on my nerves. Make me

sick. Trying to map out what I s'pose to do. With her ole buck-teeth self think she so smart and all. "I ain't putting my money with hers." I points my finger straight at Maybaby.

"Looka here, gal, you don't mean nothing to me neither. Anyways, you ain't nobody to be putting nothing with nohow. I'm only doing this for I'Lee. So you can suit yourself."

"And I ain't no gal. Gal in the cowpen named Sally Jane. So there."

"Annie Rye, we ain't got time for this." Now Doris jumping all over me for nothing. "Fussing and fighting amongst ourselves. We all hafta chip in so's Daddy can play ball week after next."

"Like I done said, I'm only doing this for I'Lee. And nobody else." Miz Flip put the last word in.

I sho feel like telling her head a mess. But I hush my mouth and listen at what Doris talking about.

"I figures ten dollars for cleaning and ironing for two weeks. And seventy-five cents for doing the barn. So that makes ten dollars and seventy-five cents."

After Doris done added it all up, I stick my chest way out. "And I got ninety-five cents."

"Even wit all that, it still won't be enough." Maybaby look right in my face. "I heard I'Lee say his suit cost round seventeen dollars."

Listen at Miz Rich Lady. What can she do about it? Come up with the rest? I'm just primping my mouth to tell her so. And I catch Doris giving me the bad eye. So I keeps my mouth shut.

"I done figured out how to make up the rest," Doris goes on to say. "Ole man Fletcher, the one Mama sell eggs to, he told me last time we was down there his wife wants to buy my quilt for six dollars. So I done made up my mind to sell it to her."

My eyes stretch wide open. "You selling your quilt you been making for your hope chest? The one you saving for your marrying? Whee-ooo. Mama gonna git you."

"She won't say nothing, 'cause I don't plan on telling her yet. Anyway, it's for a good reason. Right?"

None of us don't say nothing.

"Right?" This time Doris raise her eyebrows up.

So all us says yeah. All except Brat. "But . . . but what about Mama?"

"Y'all better pray she don't find out. Else she gonna have a fit. And more than likely it'll be on us." Maybaby go to telling us something we already know.

"We'll have to face that when we come to it," Doris say. "We all in this here together. Right?"

Nobody says yeah out loud. Just sort of mumble under they breath. So Doris put her hand up in the air. "Right hand to God."

So all us put ours up too. Just like Doris.

"Now," she says, "we gotta watch out so's no-body won't catch on to what we doing. Keep it to yourself. 'Cause we don't want Daddy to know until we surprise him."

All us say we not gonna say nothing. Not a mumbling word. Brother said it too. But I'm not believing him one bit. 'Cause he bound to be running his mouth. And sho nuff, soon as we at the table next morning, he fixing to blab everything. So I kicks at him under the table. So's he'll hush up. On top of that, when we at Miz Nettie's he start running his mouth again. So I hunch him with my elbow. Miz Nettie looks like she knowed we up to something. But she don't act nosy or nothing. She just turn the other way and go on back in the house.

A WEEK and a half done gone by, when Miz Nettie sent word she won't be needing us no more. Her regular girl coming in tomorrow. Seems her mama feeling a mite better.

All us go to looking like sick chickens.

"Ahhh, shoot." I stomps my foot. "What we s'pose to do now? It's already Wednesday. And the mailman s'pose to come on Saturday."

"How could Miz Nettie do this to us? It ain't fair. It just ain't." Doris eyes all watery. "Now everything's all messed up."

"Miz Nettie can hire out anybody she pleases,"

Mama reminds us. "And y'all don't have no say-so, one way or the other. Furthermore, I want to know what's going on around here. And there's no use trying to be sly with it. 'Cause you know I'm bound to find out sooner or later."

So Doris go on and tell Mama about what we was aiming to do.

"You mean to tell me y'all went behind my back and done something like this?"

"Mit, we didn't mean no harm."

"Listen here, Miz Lady. Y'all just gitting too grown around here. Taking matters into your own hands. I have half a mind to tell your daddy about this. Sneaking around and going on."

"But, Mama—" Doris cut in.

"No ifs, ands, or buts. I don't know what I'm gonna do with the lot a ya." Mama walk across the floor, shaking her head. "Lord knows I done my best to raise you up proper. And I never thought I'd live to see the day when my own younguns would go sneaking behind my back."

All us hang our heads down. We in real hot water now. Mama got her hands on her hips and is tapping her foot on the floor.

"Now I'm gon' figure out what to do about all this. Annie Rye . . ."

"Ma'am." I set up straight right quick.

"You gonna be put in the chicken coop."

Mer-cy, I thinks to myself. Doomsday.

"And I want you to gather all them eggs to sell to Mr. Fletcher. So we can pay for I'Lee's suit on Saturday."

"You mean it, Mama? You really mean it?" I sees a smile in Mama's eyes. And I know she means it. Every last word. So all us start jumping around, hugging on each other. And hugging on Mama.

THE NEXT DAY, after Mama gone to the field, Maybaby start aggravating me, trying to tell me what to do.

"Annie Rye, you been setting around here all morning doing nothing. You better go git them eggs up. I know you ain't done it yet. Didcha?"

I look at her like she crazy and says, "Who wants to know?"

"Look here, girl. I'm just trying to save you from gitting a whipping when Mit comes back."

"Oh, yeah. Sho you is, Maybaby. Well, for your information, I don't need you to save me from nothing. Take care of your ownself."

"Don't go gitting all huffy wit me. You best try and listen to somebody and gon' and git them eggs out that henhouse."

"Stop rushing me. Anyways, you ain't my boss. So don't be trying to tell me what to do. I'll go do it when I'm good and ready. And keep your nose outa my business."

"Then gon' witcha funny-looking self."

"Gon' to tend to my biz-ness and leave yourn alone." I make a ugly face at Maybaby and strut on out the front door. I'll show her. Just you watch. Trying to tell me what to do. Huh. I'll do just what I want to. And I'm going fishing. Soon as I find Brother, so I can talk him into digging some worms while I hunt for some safety pins to hook 'em. 'Cause the quicker I make it down to the creek, the quicker I can put my pole in the water.

When I catch up to Brother, he setting up under the black walnut tree. So I stroll up real easy like, acting as if it don't matter if I go or not.

"Think I'll go fishing."

"You is?" Brother stop playing in the dirt.

"Yep. Soon as I git my fishing pole."

"Can I come too?"

I hunch my shoulders up. "Maybe."

Brother start looking all pitiful. "Can I? Huh, Annie Rye? Can I?"

"OK," I tells him. "If you dig the worms."

I didn't have to keep begging Brother neither. Before I have my words out good, he underneath the porch dragging the hoe out. Now I aim to sneak in the house while Doris tending to Elouise. 'Cause I know she'll have something to say. Just like Maybaby. So I ease in the bedroom and take some safety pins from my cigar box and slip on out the door. Then me and Brother grab our poles and haul tail down the path. Doris go to hollering something after us, but I can't make out nothing she saying. 'Cause I done already betted Brother I can outrace him to the fishing hole. And before me and Brother have ourself situated good, them ole mudfish go showing out a good fashion, doing the somersault and flicking they tails in the air.

Brother slings his line way out. And time it hit the water, he got hisself a fish. A real big one. And he start jumping around, hooping and hollering. So I tells him to "s-s-sh," but it don't do no good. 'Cause time he hook another one, he do the same thing all over again. So I wade out where the water is just knee deep, and they pulling good, sho nuff. And before we know it, me and Brother done caught us a right smart of 'em. So me and him head on back towards the house. Then my left eye start jumping. And I knowed something gonna happen, 'cause that's a bad sign for sho. I hand Brother the fish so's he can dump them in the washtub. And I light out for the chicken coop. I just had a feeling Mama was home and was going to skin me alive about them eggs.

By the time I make it where the chickens at, they squawking up a storm. Uh-ooh. Mama already in the henhouse. And I knows I'm in real hot water this time. So I push the door open real easy like and peep in. "Mama, I was just fixing to—" My breath git hung in my throat and swell up like a big knot. Great day in the morning! Oak runners! I wheel around and nearly about trip over myself gitting up the back steps. "Dor-is! Snakes eating the eggs up!"

chapter 11

Money Music

>>>>>>>>>>>>>>>>>>>>>>>>>>>>>>>>>>>>>>>

I CATCH SIGHT of Doris soon as I make it to
the living room. She just standing out there on the
porch, gazing in the window like a frozen statue.
"Girl, what ail you?" I say. "Come on. Git the hoe."
All Doris do is motion for me to hush. And I figures it must be on account of Elouise still sleeping.
So I go tipping across the floor, and she start
pointing over where the chimney's at. And I almost
jump clean out my skin. Big ole snakes just coming
down the chimney. I look straight at Doris. And
she cut her eyes over to the corner. Oh, Lordy. A
snake crawling right up 'longside of where Elouise
laying. My legs feeling flimsy as flapjacks. Mama
done told me about them oak runners. How when

they smell milk they'd crawl straight down a youngun's throat and choke them to death.

By the time Doris inch all the way through the window, that snake already got his head weaving about Elouise's shoulder. And he steady sliding, licking his tongue out. My knees go to shaking like a leaf on a tree, and my feet won't come unloose from the floor, and Doris acting like that frozen statue again, all hunched over Elouise. All the time that ole oak runner steady easing right upside Elouise neck. I hold my breath so tight, I feels like I'm never gon' breathe no more. And before I figure out what Doris up to, she snatch Elouise up and jump out the window. Now my feet come unloosen and I take off straight out the front door, just like a streak of lightning. Straight 'cross the road. Didn't even see Mr. Tom Gifford walking up. Almost knocked that match stem down his throat.

"Whoa there, gal. Where you going in such a hurry?"

I try to tell him about them snakes being all over everyplace. But he's not making sense out nothing I'm saying, 'cause my words come out all jumbled up. So Doris tells him what done happened. The next thing I know, he done got the hoe from Brother and going in the door.

Elouise done woke up now. And she go to whimpering. Water rise up in my eyes. I'm about to cry too.

"Everything gon' be all right, Annie Rye." Doris got Elouise slung over her hip with one arm, and she scrunch me up next to her with the other one. "Y'all hush now."

But I can't hush. I just can't. Mr. Tom coming out the house with a whole bunch of dead snakes dangling over the hoe, and I let out a holler. He dump them in the wheelbarrow Daddy keep on the side of the house and tells me there's nothing to be worried about. And he tells Doris to fetch him some tin tubs and some old rags. Doris hand me Elouise and bring the tubs and the rags from out back. My legs so weak I just sit on the ground while he set the rags on fire in the tubs, then drag them in the house. Pretty soon smoke pouring out the windows and everyplace.

"This oughta drive 'em out from where they hid," Mr. Tom says, holding the hoe ready. And for real, some crawl out the window and he chop them with the hoe. I tells him about the snakes in the hen-house too.

Brother standing over next to the wheelbarrow, pointing at the nasty things. "Whee-ooo, Annie Rye, lookit that one. He a big one, ain't he?"

I just know I'm gon' puke up for sho. My stomach churning like butter. So I turn my back and face the road, and Brother call me a scarety cat.

But I don't pay him no attention. I just try to keep my mind off what's going on. But it don't do no good, 'cause I hear Mr. Tom telling Doris he gonna take them snakes on out back and bury them, soon as he git the ones in the henhouse. And that before long the smoke will die down. Then the house oughta be fit for us by the time we ready to go to sleep.

Sleep. He must be outa his mind. I'm not setting one foot in that house. Let alone talking about sleep. I'd be better off out here under the black walnut tree.

Near sundown, when Mama and Daddy come home, that's where I'm setting at. Right up under that there tree. And I don't aim to move one peg neither. But Mama tells me I should come on in the house, 'cause it can be pretty dark out here at night. And anyway, people who got good sense don't go around sleeping on the ground when they got beds to sleep in.

I don't say nothing. I don't even move. I just set there staring out across the road. Daddy must've figured it out and knowed what was the matter, 'cause he catch me by the hand.

"There ain't no cause to be scared, Stompee. Tell you what," he says, squatting down. "I'll stay up all night and keep watch, just to make sho none ain't hid noplace. How will that be?"

I nod my head, and we gon' in. But I don't hardly

sleep a wink. I was up watching. Eyeballing for them snakes. Every time I think about it the next morning, it gives me the shivers. And I feel all sick on the stomach. And if that ain't enough, Maybaby gon' to blabbing everything to Mama about what went on yesterday.

"I told her not to go fishing. She'd better do her work."

Mama cut her eyes at me. "Annie Rye, is that the truth?"

"Maybaby, you never told me no such thing. You didn't even know nothing about it. So shut your mouth."

"I sho told you to git them eggs up before Mit got home. And you start showing out. Acting like you grown. Now Ira won't have his suit today. And it's all your fault. You so stupid."

"That's enough, Maybaby. Nothing can be done about it now. I'Lee just won't be able to play tomorrow," Mama says.

"I didn't intend for the eggs to be ate up." I look down at the floor. "I didn't mean to be gone that long—just until me and Brother . . . and when I got back . . ."

"Annie Rye," Mama says, gitting up off the bed, "we'll take this matter up later. And when I git ahold of you, I'm gon' pay you up for old and new. Mark my words."

Time Mama turn her back, Maybaby leans over

in my ear. "See what you git. I hope Mit whip you clean into next week. Goody for ya. Now."

"I hate you, Maybaby. I don't care what Grandma says. I wish you'd never come to our house. Why don't you go back where you come from?" I hollers it right in her face and run out the room, water rolling down my face. Evil, that's what she is. Her real name oughta be Evil-lyn instead of Evelyn.

I want Daddy to have his suit just as much as the next one do. But Maybaby making like I don't, and now everybody all mad at me. Just you wait. One day she gonna git what's coming to her. Pow. Right on her fat lip. Huh. Mama always talking about how she needs time to git use to us. But Maybaby don't care about nobody but her ownself. Mama says, too, she need to spend more time with them. She in there now, helping Doris finish up her quilt. It don't make no sense. Them being in such a hurry and all. Mr. Fletcher done already paid the six dollars. And I figured on Mama being done by now. 'Cause she promised me a long time ago she would show me how to make some tea cakes. Even before she promised them.

But there's no use trying to make Mama change her mind. She's not listening at nothing I'm saying. Especially since Maybaby done messed everything up.

"Shoot," I mumbles under my breath, going back in the kitchen. "Mama been doing something for somebody else all day. First she fix Maybaby's hair with the straightening comb. Now she doing something with Doris. Seems like I'll never have a chance to do nothing." I rub some meat grease on my legs, the way I seen Great-Grandma Moriah do, 'cause they looking all ashy. And all a sudden Brother come ripping through the kitchen like a wild bucking horse. Nearly about knock me down.

"Brother, look where you going."

"I is. You just in my way."

I step to the other side so's he can come by. "You wanna go for a ride on my seesaw I made?" I says, trying to be nice. But he go and git all smart.

"Naw. I gonna shoot me some marbles."

"OK then, come on, so's I can show you my new spit shot."

I'm fixing to follow Brother outdoors, when he push back on my arm. "Nope. Just me and Brat. You didn't wanna show me your ole spit shot before now. You said it was a big secret. And you was gon' sell it to the President for a zillion dollars." Brother turns his nose up. "Brat gonna show me something better than yourn. Now."

Before I have a chance to tell Brother off, Mama hollers for me to see who at the door.

"It's the mailman," I hollers back. All us pile around the front door, and Mama tells us to move over, so's that white man can come on in the house.

"Howdy, Mit."

"Mr. Burley."

"Sho is a bit stifling outside." Mr. Burley fans at his corn-color hair. "Must be gon' have some rain hereabouts."

"You want something to drink? Brat, go fetch Mr. Burley a drink of water."

"Naw. Don't want to bother ya none."

"Ain't no bother," Mama says. But she sees he done made up his mind. So she go to talking about something else. "How's life serving you these days, Mr. Burley?"

But I'm not thinking none about that. My eyes fasten on that package he got tucked underneath his arm. And all us standing around looking like sick chickens. 'Cause we all knows when he walk out the door, Daddy's suit do too. But they not paying that no never mind. They just keep right on talking.

"To tell ya the truth, Mit, rheumatis gone to acting up. You wouldn't happen to have any of that tonic, would ya?"

"Can't say if I do. Annie Rye, your grandma sent any tonic when you was there a while back?"

"I gotta look, Mama. Seems like we done used it all."

"Well, gon' and see. Mr. Burley don't have all day."

"I'd be much obliged if you'd let me have a bottle or two. If you have a bit to spare."

"This here all we got," I says, holding up two bottles. "And 'nother one half empty."

"I'd be willing to pay ya a fair price. Say fifty cents for the whole lot."

Mama go back to her stitching. "Well, Mr. Burley, that's the last bit we got. And Brother, he been suffering with worms lately, and I declare I don't see no way—"

"I'd be willing," Mr. Burley cuts in, "like I done said, to make it worth your while."

Mr. Burley go to rambling in his pocket. "Will two dollars do?"

"I'd say that'll do right nicely." Mama got a grin in her eyes, so I know she up to something she not saying nothing about.

"Here you be." Mr. Burley hands Mama two one-dollar bills.

I'm standing next to Brat, and she start hunching me in my side. Mama see what she doing and make her go bring a paper sack for Mr. Burley's tonic.

"By the way, Mit, I got this here package for Ira Lee. Come all the way from Atlanta."

"Doris, take that package from Mr. Burley and fetch him his money." Mama hand Doris the two dollars Mr. Burley done give her. And all us tag behind Doris. All but Maybaby. She still propped against the wall, where she was when Mr. Burley first come in. I look over at her, and she roll her eyes at me. So I gon' and watch while Doris take the money from underneath the mattress and add it all in. The part she got for selling her quilt, the part we made at Miz Nettie's, and the two one-dollar bills Mr. Burley just give us.

"How much we got?" Brat and Brother says one after the other.

Doris looks up and gives us the eye. And so all us know everything done come out OK. Brat start jitterbugging with Brother. Acting all wild. And me and Doris hop in and do just like them.

"Y'all hush all that racket in there. And come on out here with Mr. Burley's money. I done told you he ain't got all day."

Doris leave out the room and hand Mr. Burley the money she done counted out. Soon as he walk down the steps, all us start hooping and hollering. Shouting all over the place. Mama too. Just like when Reverend Jackson done preached real good. But not Maybaby. She didn't move one peg. She still leaning up against the wall. Mama ask her what the matter is. If she sick or something. And Maybaby just twist her mouth to one side and hunch her shoulders up. So Mama says if you can't open your mouth and talk, I guess there ain't nothing the matter. But you could tell Mama didn't believe her none, 'cause she still studying on Maybaby and she don't even much pay attention to Brother jerking on her apron.

"Can we, Mama? Huh? Can we?"

"Can you what?" Mama look at Brother like she don't know what he talking about.

Brother point at the brown wrapping on the table. "Can we see it now?"

Mama says we can, so Doris go ahead and undo the package. And there it sets. Daddy's baseball suit. Spanking brand-new. Blue pants with yellow stripes running down the side. And a shirt and cap to match.

"Hot dog!" Brother snap his fingers. "Wait till Daddy come home. Boy oh boy oh boy!"

"And he'll be here pretty soon," Mama reminds us. "So y'all go finish up your work, while I put this in a good hiding place."

Mama didn't have to tell me no whole bunch of times neither. I take right off to the hogpen, so's I can be all done real quick. That is, if Brother quit slowpoking. Dragging back there toting that water.

"Brother, walk up. You slower than Christmas. And I got to go bring that other bucket of slop soon as I dump this one out in the trough." Who ever heard of a hog not eating unless she got soupy slop? That's how Daddy's new hog is. Wit her snooty self. Acting like she more than she is. Miz Upperity. "Brother, you listening at me? Make haste."

"I'm trying to. This water keep on sloushing on my britches."

"Ahhh, Brother, quit being such a big baby and hand me that bucket." Just as I'm fixing to dump the water in the hog trough, I sees something I ain't never saw in all my born days. The biggest, juiciest bait I ever laid eyes on. And I know I'd better grab that joker right now. Else he gon' git clean away. And I won't be able to find him when I want to. So I go hunting for a tin can to put him in, and first thing I know, Maybaby standing right over me.

"Annie Rye, what you doing out here fooling around? I should've knowed you'd be somewhere dodging your work. This slop bucket been setting outside the back door all morning. You know you s'pose to feed I'Lee's hogs. We ain't here to wait on you. We ain't your slaves, scatterbrain."

"You oughta leave her alone. Her brains ain't scattered. They just as good as yourn." Brat comes up behind Maybaby.

"So now you on her side, huh." Maybaby start rolling her eyes at Brat. "Well, from now on keep your liver lips out my business. 'Cause you about as stupid as the day is long."

"You stop picking at Brat, you ole mean thing," I say.

"Make me."

"You been made one time. If I make you again, you'll be home made."

Maybaby set the slop bucket down and jump right up in my face, just puffing.

"Stop blowing your breath in my face," I hollers at her.

"I'll do more than blow breath in your face."

"Oh, yeah?"

Maybaby shoves me. "Yeah."

"If you so big and bad, come across this line." I start drawing a line in the dirt, but before I'm done, Maybaby over on my side.

"Now whatcha gon' do?"

I lays a stick on my shoulder. "Knock it off. I double dare ya."

Maybaby knocks the stick off my shoulder and shoves me up against the hogpen. So I kicks her on her leg and jump over the fence.

The next thing I know, Doris telling me to bring myself from amongst them hogs. "Y'all better quit this mess out here. Passing licks and going on."

"She started it first." Maybaby go to telling her stories again. "Annie Rye just think she so much 'cause she been staying here wit Mit and I'Lee. But she ain't so much, wit her nappy-head self. All them 'BB shots spring-back knots.' " Water comes up in Maybaby's eyes, and her words come spilling out. "Wha-what we got. Nothing. If it hadn't been for Moriah, no telling what woulda become of us. Mit just walked off and left us. Ain't even cared if we lived or died."

"That's not so, Maybaby. And don't go talking like that." Doris grab hold to Maybaby's arm, and Maybaby snatch it back.

"It is too. And you know it. So ain't no use you

trying to tell me nothing. You hear. Nothing." Water go to rolling all down Maybaby's face. "Then Mit went and had little nappy-head over there. Now we left out in the cold. I'Lee her daddy. Not mine. But you watch. One day I'm gon' find my daddy. He lives right in Mitchell County. His name's James, and you just watch. One day . . ." Maybaby crying real hard now. And I get all choked up. Doris try to hug her, but she push Doris out the way and run off in the weeds.

Later on, Mama want to know where Maybaby is. So Brat tells her what went on and how Maybaby run off down the hill and all. Then Mama gits that far-off look on her face, like she looking at something nobody else can see.

MAMA GO OUT to hunt for Maybaby, so's they could straighten things out. Maybaby say she want I'Lee to take her back to Moriah's. And she ain't gon' set foot in this house never again. 'Cause if she was to drop dead tomorrow, nobody'd care. Nobody except Moriah.

Mama try to tell her that's not so. But Maybaby's not believing a word she saying.

"You left us wit Moriah so's you could go off and marry I'Lee. When y'all come back, Moriah says we ought not to stay wit y'all for a while, until you have us a place set up. Y'all must've never got no-place set up. 'Cause we been wit Moriah all this time. And you didn't even think to come and say 'here, dog' or nothing. We don't belong here." Maybaby got shaking in her voice. "We don't belong nowhere."

"Listen to me, Maybaby," I hears Mama say after I'm gone to bed. "Every time I'd come for y'all, Moriah would say to me, 'Y'all gon' now. These younguns will be just fine. Y'all got enough to start off wit. Wait until you got yourselves straighten out.' It ain't like I didn't want ya. But when Moriah got something set in her head, a team of wild horses can't drag it out. And I always figured she knowed best. She raised me. She the closest thing to a mama I ever had. My own mama passed away when I was just a baby. And I always minded Moriah's words. So if you feel like I done turned my back on you, it was never done on purpose. That's why I made up in my mind to bring y'all home to be with me. To be a family. Y'all mean just as much to me as Annie Rye and the rest of 'em." Mama wipe her eyes on her sleeve. The last thing I hear is Maybaby sniffling around in the dark in our room.

First thing this morning, I try to look Maybaby in the face, so I can figure out what she got on her mind. But she won't even look this way. Shoot. We s'pose to be having a good time. Daddy gonna git to see his brand-new suit. And play ball and everything. But nobody's in too good a mood. Got they face all tied up. Acting like they done bit down on a half-ripe persimmon. 'Specially Maybaby. On the way to church and back, all she do is gaze out the car window. Daddy says the cat got her tongue. And he says more than likely he got Brother's too. 'Cause he ain't hardly said two words all day. Boy, Daddy should've never mentioned nothing about that. 'Cause now Brother done got all wound up.

"Know what, Daddy?"

"What?"

"All us done—"

Doris clamp her hands over Brother's mouth just in time. He fixing to blab everything.

"What was you about to say, Brother?" Daddy look back over his shoulder. "You been fidgeting all day. What's wrong witcha?"

"He just gotta pee." Doris still got her hands over Brother's mouth. So he just nod his head and grunt.

Time Daddy pull up in the yard, Brat drag Brother out the car. "You best go to the outhouse and wet, before you be in a real bad tight."

A little while later, Brother come ripping in the house like a buck rabbit. Brat right behind him.

"Y'all done showed him yet?"

"Brother, hush." Doris try to quiet him down. But it don't do no good.

Brother goes right up to Daddy and pull on his britches. "They showed you yet?"

"Showed me what?"

Before Brother have a chance to open his mouth

again, I hear Mama say "I'Lee." All us look around, and there's Mama standing in the door, Daddy's baseball cap on her head and she holding up the suit.

Daddy's mouth drop wide open. And he just keep gazing at that suit.

"You like it, Daddy? Huh? You like it?" Brother go to flapping his arms like chicken wings.

"I'd say I like it a whole heap. But how . . . who . . . where in the world this come from?"

"The younguns all worked and chipped in. They knowed how much your heart was set on playing in that game this evening."

"Go ahead, hold it up against ya. So we can see how you look." Doris take the suit from Mama and hand it to Daddy.

"This is mighty fine. Mighty fine." Daddy place the shirt up next to him. "And I'm mighty proud of y'all for pulling together like this. There can't be no finer bunch of younguns this side of Georgia." Daddy lays the shirt down on the chair and pick up the britches.

"You gon' be slicker than a spit shine on a Saturday night." I looks up at Daddy, just grinning.

Daddy plop his cap on Brother's head and sling me around. "You sho nuff know it too, Stompee. Not that I can git any better-looking than I already is."

All us laugh. All except for Maybaby. She over

there looking down at the floor. And before I know it, she done eased out the room, and Elouise done eased up on the chair where Daddy shirt at.

"Git down from there, girl," I say. "Got your nasty fingerprints all over Daddy's brand-new suit."

Elouise hold her hands out and say some gibberish.

"What you been in? Syrup! Girl, you all the time in something you ain't got no business. Bring yourself on here so's I can clean you up."

Elouise don't pay me no mind. She just wobbles over and set on Daddy's foot.

"No harm done," Daddy says, picking her up. "Mit can wipe it off wit a wet rag and hang it on the line. Won't take no time to blow dry. As for you, young lady—give your pappy some sugar."

"You just done ruint that gal," Mama says, taking his shirt in the kitchen. "Annie Rye, you come on and hang this shirt out to dry. The rest of y'all git the picnic box packed." Mama runs a wet rag over Daddy's shirt and hand it to me. "You know where Maybaby at?"

"No'm. The last I saw, she was heading out the door."

"Soon as you pin that shirt on the line, you go look for her. We oughta be leaving here before long," Mama tell me.

I hollers and hunt all over the place but can't find Maybaby nowhere.

Mama come on out the house. "Where on earth could that gal be? It's no time to be playing hide-and-seek. She know we hafta git ready for the game."

"Maybe she went to Tom Gifford's house."

"Your daddy done been up there already. They ain't seen her. She ain't been herself since last night. She just been moping around. Acting like ain't nobody else in the world 'cept for her."

Mama gaze out across the field, thinking to herself, with that same look she done had before. Like there something out there will help her straighten this all out. I been had it on my mind too. And for the life of me, I can't see why Maybaby done run off like this. How she figure Mama don't care nothing about her? Shoot. Mama been spending more time with her than she is with me. And here we all is about to miss the whole game, picnic and everything. And Daddy talking about he's not going one step until Maybaby turns up. If something don't happen pretty soon, it won't be no use in even now going.

I fix the prop under the line where Daddy shirt hanging at. And here comes Miz Upperity strutting by. Just as pretty as you please. I declare, Daddy's new hog is nothing like Miz Soota, except she done got out that pen. And I best try to hem her off. So I take off behind her, and she haul tail amongst the weeds.

Mama hollers after me. But I can't make out a

word she saying, 'cause I'm already halfway down the hill.

"Bring yourself back here, hog. Where you think you going?"

Miz Upperity don't pay me no mind at all. She just keep right on heading towards the woods. So I cut betwixt some pine trees where I done seen her go. And there's no sign of her. Hide nor hair.

"Sou-eee-e. Sou-ee-e. H-e-r-e pig, pig, piggy. Bring yourself on here, hog. Shoot now. I got me something else to do beside being out here in these woods all day." I chunks down by the creek and stomp my foot.

I knows one thing. She better not have herself where I think she is. But knowing that hog ain't got the sense she was born with, I figures that's what she done did. So I go ahead and sneak down in boggy bottom. Me and Brother neither one not s'pose to. 'Cause this where them rattlesnakes be bedding down. And Brother done nearly about got hisself bit once before trying to pick him some of them pond lilies growing over yonder. That's where I spected that hog'll be. But she's noplace in sight. So I make my way on back up the slope where I was before. Then some bushes start shaking. And I knows it must be Miz Upperity. She sho won't be slipping off this time. No sir.

"Miz Upperity," I says, parting the bushes back. "Take yourself— Maybaby! Girl, what you doing?

We been looking all over the place for you. How come you squatting down here shaking these bushes?"

Maybaby put her finger up to her mouth so I'll hush. But I can't figure out why she acting the way she doing. Holding herself all stiff. Like she in a tight and don't have time to make it to the outhouse. So I says, "Girl, what's ailing you?"

Maybaby don't even now open her mouth. She just point down at the creek. Then I see Miz Upperity stuck in the mud, halfway up to her back. "Come on, girl, what you standing here gazing in space for? Let's go pull her out." I'm just fixing to take off, and Maybaby hold me back.

"Listen," she says, all quiet like.

Now I hears it too. Sound just like teeny rocks jiggling in a glass jar. And I knows what it is. Now I see why Maybaby was shaking them bushes to bring me over here. A snake. A big rattlesnake weaving through some sticks flicking his tongue out. And he a short piece from Miz Upperity.

"What we gon' do, Annie Rye?" Maybaby's voice go to quivering.

"Chunk this here rock and knock his head off." I draws back my arm, and my legs git weak as water.

"What's the matter?"

"I'm scared I gon' miss."

"You not gonna miss. You can chunk good."

Now we both talking down real low.

"But I can't be still. My knees keep on knocking."

"Move this way a little bit, so's I can hold you steady." Maybaby bend down and grab me around my legs.

But I'm still scared. Great day in the morning, I'm scared now. That there snake done turned and heading straight for Miz Upperity. Now Maybaby go to squeezing my legs real tight.

"Dip-see-do, Annie Rye, dip-see-do."

I chunks just as hard as I can. And that snake pop up in the air and hit the ground.

"He dead, Annie Rye?" Maybaby's voice shaking real bad now.

Me and her latch on to each other. "I can't say if he is or if he ain't," I say, still keeping my voice down. "I just know we best watch our step. And don't make no noise."

Me and Maybaby creep up a piece, so's we can take us a good look. 'Cause he might be playing possum or something. When we nearly about up on him, I jab him with a stick.

"Yeah, he dead."

"Sho nuff is. Good and dead. You got him right between the eyeballs. And he about to make me sick-on-the-stomach." Maybaby pick up a stick, and me and her drag him off in the bushes.

"Now how Miz Upperity gon' git unstuck?" I says when we all done.

"Come on," says Maybaby. "You pull from the front and I push from the back."

"Okay. But lemme git a good hold first." I wrap my arms around Miz Upperity's neck, and every time I have me a good hold, she wiggle her head loose.

"Annie Rye, you pulling?"

"I'm trying to. But this here hog won't act right."

"Then come on back here where I'm at, and you and me both can push."

I go on the other side next to where Maybaby is. We almost push our gizzards out. And Miz Upperity still not budging. Not one bit. "Girl, this here hog too fat to be pushing on. Pretty soon our eyeballs gonna pop out."

"She heavy all right. So when I count to three, you and me push at the same time."

I give Miz Upperity a hard shove time Maybaby say "Push!" and Miz Upperity go squealing out towards the path, and I'm pulling my face out the mud. Maybaby is too. Me and her look at each other and can't do nothing but laugh.

"Annie Rye, girl, you look just like a big ol' mud pie."

"You look like one that got two big eyes peeping out."

Now we grinning all over again, trying to pull up on each other. And we slip right back down. Still laughing. Then me and Maybaby see it at the same time. Another rattlesnake. He just setting over there shaking his tail.

"Come on here, Maybaby. Let's git."

Quick as anything, me and her crawl out on our hands and knees and haul tail up the hill.

Soon as we come to the edge of the woods, there's Miz Upperity rooting in some weeds.

"Git on home, hog," I hollers at her. "Scat."

Miz Upperity don't waste no time heading towards the house. And me and Maybaby take off after her. That hog not paying no attention to what she doing and run smack dab into the prop. The clothesline fall down and Daddy's baseball shirt with it.

By now everybody in the backyard looking at me and Maybaby like we crazy or something.

"Maybaby. What y'all been up to? Just look at yourself!" Mama put her hand on her hip. "Mercy. What will y'all be into next?"

"But . . . ," me and Maybaby says at the same time.

"No ifs, ands, or buts about it," Mama goes on. "Y'all done drove that hog up here and tore down my clothesline and got your daddy's shirt filthy. Maybaby you old enough to know better."

Maybaby don't say nothing. She just hang her head down and start scraping mud off her knees.

So I speak up right fast. "Miz Upperity got bogged down in the mud. And a snake was coming, and I . . . we . . ." I try to tell Mama how it was, but

I git all mixed up. So I cut my eyes down at the ground. "It was much my fault as hers."

"Oh, it was, huh? Well, don't worry, young lady. You won't be gitting off so easy neither." Mama act like she's not believing a word I done said. So Daddy try to take up for us.

"Ah, Mit. Don't be so hard on 'em. Give 'em the benefit of the doubt. I don't think they meant for it to turn out the way it did. Look at all that mud. It done already went to caking up on 'em. Pretty soon they won't be able to pry it loose with a chisel. Anyways, the hog back in the pen and the board nailed back. So why don't we just leave it at that?"

Mama turns to Daddy. "Whether I give 'em the benefit or not, I'Lee, there's no way that shirt will be ready before we hafta leave for the game. I'll rinse it out and wring it in a sheet. And Doris can press over it with the smoothing iron. But it still ain't gon' be halfway dry enough to wear noplace. We'd be better off just to stay on home."

"Stay home!" All us cry out at the same time.

"You mean after all we done, Daddy still not gonna have a chance to play in his new baseball suit?" Brat say.

"And how's it s'pose to dry?" Mama snap at her. "By magic? And just look at Maybaby and Annie Rye. Covered with mud from head to toe." Mama was plain disgusted. I could tell by the way she flung her arms in the air.

So I just hang my head down and scratch at the mud itching my leg. Shucks. I sho done messed everything up good this time. With my know-it-all self. Mama done told me, I don't know how many times, "That little piece of red flannel in your mouth gon' be your ruin." I know I'm fixing to cry, so I walk off where the washtubs setting at, so nobody won't see. Then I hear Daddy call my name.

"Stompee, come on back here. We not gon' lay the blame on nobody," Daddy says to me like he done read my mind. "Sometimes things just don't come out the way we plan 'em. But it makes me feel good what y'all done. It makes me proud that y'all think enough of me to go through all this bother so I'd have a chance to play. And I want y'all to know it, doggone it. I said it many a times and I say it again. Y'all the best set of younguns anybody could ask for. And Mit"—Daddy turn to Mama—"we's going to the game. Suit or no suit."

Mama open her mouth to say something. But Daddy tells her no ifs, ands, or buts about it. We going. So Mama don't say another word. Daddy done put his foot down. Done said what he meant. And that was all there was to it.

"Now," Daddy goes on, "it ain't the end of the world. I know it's the first game of the season, but there'll be some more I can play in."

"Not like this one," Doris butts in. "Y'all s'pose

to be playing against the baddest team in Mitchell County."

"Ahhh, Daddy. Why can't you just pitch wit no suit on?" Brat say. "Just this one time?"

" 'Cause that's the rule, Brat. But that's no reason for us to go moping around. The main thing is y'all pulled together on this thing. And we don't aim to let nothing or nobody spoil it. So we going to the game, and we gonna have us a good time. And I don't want to see no more long faces. You hear?"

"Phu-eee." Brother stomps his foot. "It ain't gonna be no fun if you ain't chunking."

"Come on now. Remember what I just said. We gonna have ourselves a good ole time. You'll see. Now y'all run along. Finish packing the fried chicken, 'tato salad, and sweet bread. Don't bother about no lemonade. We all gonna have us some soda water. We can stop at Pete's on the way. They open on Sunday." Daddy slap his hands together. "So git a-moving."

Doris and them go on and do like Daddy done said. All except for me and Maybaby. We got to go git washed up in the tin tub setting alongside the house. I knowed we was gonna be leaving directly. So I step in and start splashing water on my legs. Maybaby step in next to me and go to whispering something in my ear. I start grinning and whisper back in hers. Me and Maybaby done got us a plan. We sho now do.

Soon as we done got everything all set, Daddy cranks the car up. And we head off towards Hopefull, where they gonna be playing ball at. We hardly out of the piney woods yet, when all of a sudden, my left eye start jumping. And I knows that's a bad sign. Something gon' happen sho as I setting here. I just knows it.

Brother inching around and squiggling like a worm in a tin can. Doris tell him to be still, and Brother screw his face up. "I wanna drink of water."

"Well, Jitterbug," Daddy says, "you just settle down back there. We oughta come across that store before long. Then while I buy the soda water, you can git yourself a swallow or two from the spigot."

Before Daddy was done talking good, we spot Pete's Wayside Grocery, setting a little ways off the highway. So Daddy pull up next to the gas pump, where a puky-green tractor standing at, and all us pile out.

chapter 12

Let Bygones
Be Bygones

>>>>>>>>>>>>>>>>>>>>>>>>>>>>>>>>>>>

WE KNOWED NOT to go roaming around all over the place, even before we set foot in the store. So I just stand in the corner where they got sawdust spread on the floor and squeeze it between my toes while I wait for Daddy to ask the store man what kind of soda water he got. Time Daddy open his mouth, a man with a big belly wheels around. Mr. Lampkins. And I could tell he madder than all git-up. 'Cause his face steaming red.

"Well, well. If it ain't the uppity nigger. I ain't forgot how you caused me to git put off Myszell's place," he says, trying to take the spite out on Daddy.

"That ain't quite the way it was, Mr. Lampkins."

"You calling me a liar, boy?" Mr. Lampkins' eyes squinches almost shut.

"Ain't calling ya nothing. The truth is the truth. But I ain't got no quarrel witcha. Just let bygones be bygones."

Mr. Lampkins says some bad cuss words and grab a pitchfork. "I'm gonna take some a that hot air out your britches. Gonna bring ya right down to size."

I'm so scared I don't know what to do. And all these white folk standing here ain't doing nothing neither. They ain't even trying to stop him or nothing. All one of them says is "Take it easy, Lampkins." But Mr. Lampkins ain't taking it easy. And they just gon' stand around and let Daddy be hurt.

Mr. Lampkins turning the pitchfork over in his hand, his eyes steady on Daddy.

I try to scream when I feel my mouth fly open. But all I hear is Mama holler out, "I'Lee." Mr. Lampkins coming at him with the pitchfork. Daddy ducks to one side and the sharp pongs catch in his sleeve. Mr. Lampkins yank it out and draw it back. And I knows Daddy gon' git hurt bad. Real bad. I know it for sho. Lord have mercy. He fixing to jab Daddy with the pitchfork.

"Hey, Lampkins!" Someone come busting in the door. "Your Sissy done fell over in the well."

Mr. Lampkins turns, dropping the pitchfork. Him and all the other white folks hurry out back. I'm shaking so bad I can hardly follow Daddy and them behind the store.

Mr. Lampkins squatting beside the well. "Sissy. Sissy, gal, you all right?" Mr. Lampkins' voice sound like he trying to hold back a cry. "Sissy, you hear me, gal?"

I thought maybe she had got drowned, until I hear some whimpering. Then I knows she ain't. That's why everybody trying to figure out how to hoist her up real quick.

"Seems to me it gonna take a lot of doing," say a old white lady. "Ain't never seen nothing akin to it."

Then a tall, skinny-looking white man, dragging on his words like he got to think up what he want to say before he say it, put in, "Wit all that loose clay and sand, it can give way anytime. Cave right in."

I see all the other white folk look at each other. And I know none of them is about to go down in that well. And I knowed, too, Mr. Lampkins wouldn't fit. His belly being so big and all.

I look over my shoulder to make sho Brother still out here where we at, and I see Daddy coming across the field, driving the tractor that was setting out front. And I knowed what was in his mind before he said it.

"I'll go down and bring her out. And I'll be

needing some rope." Daddy look off in the crowd of white folk.

I cut my eyes up at Mama. By the look on her face, I can tell she don't want Daddy to go. But she knows Daddy done already got his mind set. So she don't even open her mouth. She just stand there waiting with the rest of us, Elouise slung over her hip.

Right quick Mr. Pete come back with some rope. Soon as they git through knocking the rotten boards from the sides of the well, he tie one end of the rope under Daddy's arms and the other to the back of the tractor. Now they let Daddy down in the well.

"A little more." Daddy's voice come up all hollow like. "I can just about reach her."

Mr. Pete back the tractor up a ways. "How's that?" he call, wiping sweat off his bald spot.

"That'll do," Daddy call up. Then I hear Daddy trying to talk that Sissy girl into turning loose that piece of root she hanging on to, so's she can grab hold to his neck. She ain't no bigger than a flea, so she oughta not weigh Daddy down too much. Now I hears him say, "Now you hold on tight." And I know he done got her.

A speckled-face man gives Mr. Pete a sign, and Mr. Pete move the tractor real slow out across the field.

"Hold it," the man yell out to Mr. Pete. "The rope caught. Back up some."

Mr. Pete back up too fast. Then I hears a big splash. Daddy done dropped all the way to the bottom of the well. My stomach flip over, and I feels Maybaby's hand latching on to mine.

"Pull 'em up! Miss Sissy gon' drown!" Mr. Lampkins yells at Mr. Pete.

At first it look like Mr. Pete couldn't make the tractor work. My throat git all knotted up. I just know he ain't gonna pull my daddy out. Then the tractor make a grinding noise and moves forward, pulling the rope slowly over the edge of the well.

Little shivers running all over my stomach. "Daddy! You OK?" He don't make no sound. And me and Maybaby hold each other's hands so tight we about to squeeze the skin off.

Doris and Brat all huddle around Mama. Brother do too. Water rising in my eyes. "Dad-dy!"

Now I hear him and that Sissy girl coughing and trying to catch they breath. And I know he OK.

Mr. Pete take the tractor all the way out by the weeds, hoisting Daddy up out of the well. All the white folks start clapping they hands and slapping Daddy across the back, saying what a good job he done did. All except for Mr. Lampkins. He just grabs that Sissy girl from hanging on to Daddy's neck and stares at him like there something about Daddy he haven't quite figured out yet. Then he just walks off. He don't open his mouth to say a mumbling word. Not even one thank-you.

But now I knowed it ain't made a bit of difference how Mr. Lampkins done treated Daddy. Daddy just went ahead and did what needed to be did. Seeing how Mr. Lampkins ain't had nobody else to do it for him. I guess it ain't good to be giving tit for tat. No telling when you might be in the same fix somebody else in. And you be the one needing. Just like Mr. Lampkins.

Daddy put on the change of clothes Mr. Pete done give him. He give us a crate of soda water too. Brung them out and put 'em right in the car. All for free. So Daddy tells him "Much obliged," and we head on towards Hopefull. That's when me and Maybaby take out Daddy's baseball stuff we done sneaked in the car and go to holding his shirt out the window, so's it'll dry by the time we git to where we going. 'Cause the Lord willing and the creek don't rise, Daddy might just make it to the game before it's all over and done with.

chapter 13

Through Thick and Thin

>>>>>>>>>>>>>>>>>>>>>>>>>>>>>>>>>>>

ON THE WAY back home, Mama and them say how smart we was for doing like we did, hanging Daddy's shirt out the car window and all. I hunch Maybaby in the side, and she hunch me back. We knowed we was slick already. Shoot. We knowed it all along. 'Cause by the time we got to where we was going, Daddy's shirt had blowed dry. And he got in the game right off.

It didn't matter none that it was halfway over. 'Cause Daddy done the best pitching you ever did wanna see. And all us was just hollering, and clapping our hands, and jumping up and going on. Daddy was striking 'em out right and left. The Boweevils was even with the Hawkeyes. It was all tied up. So I hollers out, "Dip-see-do." Daddy cocked his hat to one side and spit tobacco juice. And I knowed they'd better watch out. 'Cause Daddy done crooked his legs and drawed his hands back. And before we knowed what was happening, that ball went flying like nobody's business. Whoop. And that was all she wrote. Struck him out quicker than you could say boo.

And all Brother been saying is "Boy oh boy oh boy!" and socking his hands together. Now he done wore hisself out, and done gone to sleep here in the back seat. Not me. I ain't a bit sleepy. No sir. Not after the Boweevils done won. Done beat 'em fair and square. I hunch Maybaby again. And she hunch me back. We look at each other just grinning and start singing "Ole MacDonald Had a Farm." Then we switch it around and go to singing "Ole man Footman had a farm, E-I-E-I-O, and on that farm he had some chillun, E-I-E-I-O. With a pigtail here, and a pigtail there, here a tail, there a tail, everywhere a piggytail . . ." I hold up one of my plaits, and Maybaby hold up one of hers. Mama and them laugh and join in too.

As we go past Mr. Pete's grocery store, I think about all what done happened to Daddy. To all us. And I wink my eye at Maybaby, and she wink right back. I guess you can do most anything when you set your mind to it. Even to being a family. And that's what we all is. Family. And that's for true.

ETHEL FOOTMAN SMOTHERS grew up as the eldest of seven in a small rural town in Georgia. With no television and few books, she entertained her brothers and sisters with made-up stories. She has been making up stories ever since. *Down in the Piney Woods* is her fictionalized recollection of those years in Camilla, Georgia.

A mother of four, a grandmother, and a published poet, Ethel Smothers lives with her husband in Grand Rapids, Michigan. This is her first novel for children.